"But our wedding night should be commemorated, should it not?" he asked.

"I don't—"

But he wasn't really asking.

His mouth came down on hers as uncompromising and hard as she remembered, as he had been since she'd met him so few hours before. This time he tasted her lips only briefly, before moving across her jaw, her temple, learning the shape of her. His mouth was hot. Gabrielle felt her own fall open in shock—in response. She felt feverish. Outside herself.

Something in her thrilled to it—to him—even as the rest of her balked at such a naked display of ownership. Her hands flew to his shoulders, though it was like pushing against stone.

Then, as suddenly, he set her away from him, a very masculine triumph written across his face.

"You are mine," he said. Claiming her.

Caitlin Crews discovered her first romance novel at the age of twelve. It involved swashbuckling pirates, grand adventures, a heroine with rustling skirts and a mind of her own, and a seriously mouthwatering and masterful hero. The book (the title of which remains lost in the mists of time) made a serious impression. Caitlin was immediately smitten with romances and romance heroes, to the detriment of her middle school social life. And so began her life-long love affair with romance novels, many of which she insists on keeping near her at all times.

Caitlin has made her home in places as far-flung as York, England, and Atlanta, Georgia. She was raised near New York City, and fell in love with London on her first visit when she was a teenager. She has backpacked in Zimbabwe, been on safari in Botswana, and visited tiny villages in Namibia. She has, while visiting the place in question, declared her intention to live in Prague, Dublin, Paris, Athens, Nice, the Greek Islands, Rome, Venice, and/or any of the Hawaiian islands. Writing about exotic places seems like the next best thing to moving there.

She currently lives in California, with her animator/comic book artist husband and their menagerie of ridiculous animals.

PURE PRINCESS, BARTERED BRIDE

BY
CAITLIN CREWS

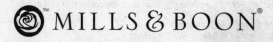

MILLS & BOON

First published in Great Britain 2009
Paperback edition 2010
Harlequin Mills & Boon Limited,
Eton House, 18-24 Paradise Road, Richmond, Surrey TW9 1SR

© Caitlin Crews 2009

ISBN: 978 0 263 87771 7

Set in Times Roman 10¼ on 12¼ pt
01-0210-53817

Harlequin Mills & Boon policy is to use papers that are natural, renewable and recyclable products and made from wood grown in sustainable forests. The logging and manufacturing process conform to the legal environmental regulations of the country of origin.

Printed and bound in Spain
by Litografia Rosés, S.A., Barcelona

PURE PRINCESS,
BARTERED BRIDE

To Jane Porter: inspiration, mentor,
and the big sister I always wanted.
Thank you, for everything.

PROLOGUE

LUC GARNIER did not believe in love.

Love was madness. Agony, despair and crockery hurled against walls. Luc believed in facts. In proof. In ironclad contracts and the implacable truth of money. He had been relentless and focused all his life and as a result, wildly successful. He did not believe this was a matter of luck or chance. Emotion played no part in it.

Just as emotion played no part in picking out his future bride.

The Côte d'Azur preened itself in the warm afternoon sun as Luc strode down a side street in Nice, headed for the Promenade des Anglais, where the famously luxurious Hotel Negresco sat in gracious Victorian splendor, looking out onto the sparkling blue waters of the Baie des Anges and the Mediterranean Sea beyond. The Hotel Negresco was one of Luc's favorite hotels in France, and thus the world, overflowing as it was with museum-quality art and a famously accommodating staff—but he had a far more pressing reason for visiting Nice's landmark hotel today.

Luc had flown in that morning from his Paris headquarters, determined to see for himself if the latest potential bride—who looked so good on paper—looked even half as good in person.

But then, they all looked good on paper, as they had to be of a noble family to so much as make his list. The last woman he had considered for the position had seemed like a perfect match on paper—but a few days spent tailing Lady Emma around her London society life had quickly revealed that the young noble-woman had a secret penchant for late nights with rough gentlemen.

It wasn't that Luc necessarily minded that his wife might have a past—he simply preferred that, whatever the past was, it had involved the sort of people who would not make interesting headlines should the tabloids catch wind of them. *Lady Emma Prefers Goths to Garnier.* He could imagine it all too well.

"That's the way modern women are these days," his number two man had told him, after Luc had discovered Lady Emma's late-night bar-crawling. Alessandro was the closest thing Luc had to a friend, but even so, he'd thrown his hands up in the air when Luc had glared at him across his opulent Paris office.

"Modern women may be as loose as they like," he'd snapped. "But my wife will not be. Is this so much to ask?"

"This is not all you ask!" Alessandro had replied with a laugh. He'd begun to tick off the necessary items on his fingers. "She must be noble, if not royal, to honor your bloodline. She must be pure in word and deed. She must never have been young or stupid, as no scandal can ever have touched her." He'd shaken his head sadly. "I do not think this woman exists."

"She may not," Luc had agreed, closing the dossier he had compiled on Lady Emma and setting it aside with distaste. "My mother taught me long ago that beauty is too often a mask for dishonor and betrayal. One cannot depend on it—only on an irreproachable reputation." He had smiled at Alessandro. "If she does exist, I will find her."

"And what if this paragon does not wish to marry you when

you have hunted her down?" Alessandro had asked dryly. "What then?"

Luc had laughed. "Please." He'd sat back in his chair and gazed at his friend, crooking his brow in amusement. "That is not very likely, is it? What woman would not benefit from becoming my wife? What can any woman possibly want that I cannot give her? I will place all of my wealth and power at the disposal of whatever woman can fill the position."

Alessandro had sighed heavily, his romantic Italian soul no doubt mortally wounded at the prospect of *filling the position* of wife. "Women like romance and fairy tales," he'd said. Luc rather thought Alessandro was the one who preferred such fripperies, but had not said so. "They do not want marriage to be conducted as a business proposition."

"But that is what it is," Luc had said, shrugging again. "The correct woman must understand this as well."

"I fear you will be looking for a very long time, my friend," Alessandro had said, shaking his head.

But Luc had never been afraid of hard, seemingly fruitless work, he reflected as he turned the corner and saw the famous façade of the Hotel Negresco before him. In fact, he thrived on it. His famous parents had died when he was barely twenty-three, and he had had to make his own way in the world in their considerable shadows. Even before their deaths in a boating accident he had been more or less on his own—his parents having been far more interested in each other and their endless romantic complications than in their son.

Luc could not bring himself to regret his unorthodox upbringing, no matter how many people seemed to think it pointed to some lack in him—something no one had dared say to his face in some time. Growing up in such a way, surrounded by so much heightened emotion mixed with jealousy and betrayal and avid outside interest, had stripped him of many of the needs that ruled other men. It had also made him that much more successful, which was all he cared about—for what else was there? He did not need the emotions that other men did. He was not interested in love, and all the upheaval and agony it brought. He wanted a wife in the most traditional sense, for the most traditional reasons. He was nearing forty now, and it was time he created a family to carry on his legacy and his mother's royal Italian bloodline. The wife he chose would have to be from an equally august bloodline—noble for centuries, at the very least, as his family was. It was tradition. It was his duty.

He needed a wife who knew her duty.

He strode into the elegant old hotel, past the white-gloved doormen, and did not bother to gape like a tourist at the sparkling lobby that emanated old French charm and elegance all around him. He had seen it many times before. The Hotel Negresco prided itself on its luxuriousness. Luc made his way toward the Salon Royal, with its Gustave Eiffel-designed dome and Baccarat chandeliers sparkling over a crowd of some of the world's foremost philanthropists. He ignored the well-dressed and genteel throng, as well as the priceless art that graced the walls. He searched the room until his eyes fell on the woman he'd been looking for—Princess Gabrielle of Miravakia.

She stood out from the crowd in a good way, he was pleased to note. She did not call attention to herself. She did not display her chest in an inappropriate manner or hang all over the men who competed for her attention. She seemed cool and elegant, refined and royal, as she stood in the center of a knot of extremely well-dressed patrons.

She was lovely—but then, she should be. She was a royal princess, after all—the heir to her country's throne. He ignored her looks and concentrated on the way she presented herself:

her public persona, which was by all accounts completely without blemish.

Her hair was swept back into an elegant knot at the nape of her neck, and she wore a simple cocktail dress with restrained hints of jewelry at her ears and one wrist. Nothing flashy or gauche. She was all sophistication and class, presiding over this great reception for one of her pet charities with all the grace for which she was known. She was every inch the perfect princess.

He liked what he saw. But he couldn't trust what she showed the world at a reception for six hundred. Could a woman really be as above reproach as this one appeared to be?

Luc signaled a passing waiter and requested a drink, then moved to the outskirts of the crowd, from where he could watch her without being observed in return. She was in Nice for the week, he knew, and was expected to make a number of appearances—which interested him less than what she got up to in her free time.

He was sure that, like Lady Emma before her, Princess Gabrielle would eventually show herself to him. He had only to wait, and watch.

But as Luc watched the perfect-looking princess make her rounds, he allowed himself a moment of cautious optimism as he sampled his drink.

If she proved to be as perfect as she looked, he had done it. He had finally found his bride.

CHAPTER ONE

"DO YOUR duty," her father ordered her only moments before the organ burst into life—his version of an encouraging speech. He frowned at her. "Make me proud."

That was the entirety of his fatherly pre-wedding advice.

The words swam in Princess Gabrielle's head even as the heavy weight of her silk taffeta wedding gown tugged at her and slowed her down. The long train swept back from her dress, extending almost ten feet behind her as befitted a royal princess on her wedding day. Gabrielle only knew that it was hard to walk with ten feet of fabric to pull along with her, though she kept her spine erect and her head high—as always.

Thank God for the veil that covered her face, hiding the expression she was afraid she couldn't control for the first time in her twenty-five years—to say nothing of the prickly heat flooding her eyes.

She could not cry. Not here. Not now.

Not as she walked down the aisle of her kingdom's holiest of cathedrals, holding fast to her father's arm. Her father—King Josef of Miravakia. The man she had spent her life trying—and failing—to please.

Even at university she had been too determined to win her father's elusive approval to do anything but study hard. While her peers had partied and explored all that London had to offer, Gabrielle had lost herself in her books and her research. After university, despite the degree she'd obtained in Economics, she had dedicated herself to charity work, according to her father's expectations of the Crown Princess of Miravakia.

Anything and everything to curry her father's favor. It was the mantra of Gabrielle's life.

Even this. Marriage to a perfect stranger of his choosing.

Why was she going through with this? Hers was not some ancient feudal kingdom—and she was no chattel. But if there was a way to go against her father's wishes without incurring his wrath she did not know what it was. She knew that she could have said no. Couldn't she? Or was she simply too desperate to prove to her father that she was worthy of his approval—even when the stakes were so high?

"I have accepted a marriage proposal," King Josef had told her one morning, barely three months ago, jolting Gabrielle from her contemplation of the day's schedule. He had not glanced up from his breakfast as he spoke. It had surprised Gabrielle that he'd spoken at all—he generally preferred to breakfast in silence, with only his newspapers spread around him, though he insisted that she join him every morning.

"A marriage proposal?" Gabrielle had been amazed—her father had shown no interest in remarrying, not in all the long years since Gabrielle's mother had died of cancer when Gabrielle was barely five.

"I found the combination of a royal bloodline and near-limitless wealth sufficiently attractive," the King had said, almost thoughtfully. "And it will certainly bolster the standing of the Miravakian throne."

It had been as if he was discussing the purchase of a vehicle. But Gabrielle's thoughts had raced ahead anyway. Was she really to have a stepmother? She rather thought it might be fun to have someone else around the *palazzo*. Much as she loved her father and tried to please him, he was not an easy man.

"There will be no tedious long engagement," he had continued, touching his thin, disapproving lips with his linen napkin and signaling one of the hovering footmen for more coffee. Finally, he'd looked at her. "I've no patience for such things."

"No, of course not," Gabrielle had agreed. Her mind had been racing wildly. Who on earth could possibly meet her father's high standards? He had a universally low opinion of almost every woman he'd ever encountered, as far as she knew—and then again, as King of Miravakia, he would only consider a bride from a select class of royals. *And how like him to keep his intentions a secret*, she'd thought, almost amused.

"I expect you to conduct yourself well," he'd said, sipping at his coffee. "None of the hysterics that seem to afflict your sex when they come into contact with a wedding ceremony, thank you."

Gabrielle had known better than to respond to that.

He'd sniffed. "I have confidence that you can put everything together quickly and efficiently, with as little disruption as possible."

"Of course, Father," Gabrielle had said at once. She had never planned a wedding before, but how different could it be from the state events she'd put together in the past? She had a marvelous staff whom she already knew could perform miracles. And who knew? Perhaps a new wife would bring out the softer side of her stern father. She'd give quite a bit to see that.

Lost in her reverie, she had been startled when her father had pushed back his chair and stood. He'd moved toward the door without another word—the subject closed. Gabrielle had almost laughed. How typical of him. She'd felt a surge of affection for his brusque ways—because clearly something romantic lurked beneath the cold exterior.

"Father," she had called, stopping him before he quit the room. He'd turned back to face her, a slight frown between his eyebrows.

"What is it?" he had asked impatiently.

"Am I to know the bride's name?" she had asked, biting back an indulgent smile.

He'd stared at her. "You need to pay closer attention, Gabrielle, if you are to succeed me without running this country into the ground," he'd snapped, his arctic tone making her wince. His frown had deepened as he'd glared at her. "*You*, obviously, are the bride."

And then he'd turned on his heel and strode from the room, without a backward glance.

In the cathedral, Gabrielle felt her breath catch in her throat as the memory of that morning washed over her, while her pulse fluttered wildly. Panic was setting in, as heavy around her as the veil she wore and the train she trailed behind her. She fought to pull air into her lungs—ordered herself to stay calm.

Her father would never forgive her if she made a scene. If she showed anything but docile acceptance—even gratitude—for the way he'd chosen to manage her affairs. Her life.

Her marriage.

Gabrielle felt the crisp, heavy sleeve of her father's ornamental coat beneath her trembling fingers as he led her down the long aisle, his measured steps bringing her closer and closer to her fate.

She couldn't think of it. Couldn't think of *him*—her groom. Soon to be her husband. A man she had never even met, and yet he would be her spouse. Her mate. King of her people when she became their queen. Gabrielle's lips parted on a sound that was far too close to a sob—though it was thankfully hidden in the swirl of music that surrounded her.

She could not. Not here. Not now. It was too late.

The cathedral was packed to capacity on all sides, filled with Europe's royals and assorted nobles. Political allies and strategic partners of her father's. The music soared toward the stained glass heights, filling the space and caressing the carved marble statues. Outside, she knew, the people of Miravakia were celebrating their princess's wedding day as a national holiday. There would be rejoicing in the streets, the papers claimed, now that their Gabrielle had found her husband. Their future king.

A man she did not know and had never seen—not in person. Not face-to-face.

Her husband-to-be was a man who had won his wife through contracts—meetings with her father, bargains struck and approved without her knowledge or consent. Her father had not asked Gabrielle for her input—he had not considered her feelings at all. He had decided that it was time she married, and he had produced the bridegroom of his choice.

And Gabrielle never argued with her father. Never rebelled, never contradicted. Gabrielle was good. Obedient. Respectful to a fault. In the hope that her father would one day respect her back. Love her, maybe—just a little.

Instead, he'd sold her off to the highest bidder.

Luc felt triumph surge through him as he watched the woman—*soon to be his wife*—walk toward him down the long ceremonial aisle. He barely noticed the arching stained glass above him as he stood at the altar, or the hunched statues of gargoyles peering down at him—his attention was focused entirely on her.

Finally.

Luc's mouth pressed into a thin line as he thought of his reckless, thoughtless mother and the destruction she had wrought with her rebellions. Her "passions." But Luc was not his temperamental, easily manipulated father. He would not stand for such behavior—not from *his* wife.

She must be above reproach. She must be practical—as this was to be a marriage on paper first and flesh afterward. But most of all she must be trustworthy. Because Luc, unlike many of his station, would not tolerate disloyalty. There would be no *discreet affairs* in this marriage. He would accept nothing less than one hundred percent obedience. There would be no tabloid speculation, no scandals for the voyeurs to pick over. *Never again.*

He'd searched for years. He'd rejected untold numbers of women before arriving at near misses like Lady Emma. As with everything in his life, from his business to the personal life he guarded ferociously, Luc's refusal to compromise had first isolated, then rewarded him.

Because he had not compromised, because he did not know the meaning of the word, he had exactly what he wanted. The perfect princess. At last.

Princess Gabrielle was biddable. Docile—as evidenced by her presence in the cathedral today, calmly walking down the aisle into an arranged marriage because her father had ordered her to do so. *So far, so good*, he thought with deep satisfaction as he watched her slow, sure approach.

He remembered the sun-drenched days when he'd followed her in Nice, her seemingly effortless poise, no matter how many clamored for her attention. She had never caused a single scandal in her life. She was known for her serenity and her complete lack of tabloid presence. When she made the papers it was in recognition of her charity work. Never for her exploits. Compared to the other royals who debauched themselves all over Europe, she might be a saint. Which suited Luc just fine.

Luc Garnier had built an empire based on his perfectionist streak. If it was not perfect, it would not carry his name.

His wife would be no different.

He had left nothing to chance. He had had others collect the initial information, but then he had made the final decision—as he always did, no matter the acquisition in question. He had followed her personally, because he knew that he could not trust anyone's opinion but his own. Not when it came to a matter of such importance. Others might make mistakes, or overlook seemingly small details that would later prove to be of importance—but not Luc. He would never have approached her father if he had not been absolutely satisfied that Princess Gabrielle was not just the best choice, but the only choice for his bride.

Luc had met with King Josef to settle the final contracts in the King's sumptuous suite at the Hotel le Bristol in Paris, with its stunning view of the great Sacré-Coeur basilica that rose, gleaming white, and towered above the city from Montmartre.

"You do not wish to meet her?" the older man had asked when the business was done, settling back in his chair to enjoy his port.

"It is not necessary," Luc had replied. He had inclined his head. "Unless you wish it?"

"What is it to me?" the King had asked, letting out a puff of air through his nose. "She will marry you whether you meet her or not."

"You are certain?" Luc had asked lightly, though he had not in truth been concerned. Arrangements would never have reached this stage if the King had not been sure of his daughter's obedience. "Ours is an unusual settlement in this day and age. A princess and a kingdom in exchange for wealth and business interests—I am told this sounds like something out of a history book."

The King had made a dismissive noise. "My daughter was

raised to do the right thing regarding her country. I have always insisted that Gabrielle understands her position necessitates a certain dignity." The King had swirled his port in its tumbler. He had frowned. "And great responsibility."

"She appears to have taken it to heart," Luc had said, looking at his own drink. "I have never heard her mentioned without reference to her grace and composure."

"Of course." The King had seemed almost taken aback. "She has known all her life that her role as princess would come before any more personal considerations. She will be a good queen one day—though she requires a firm hand to guide her." He'd sniffed. "You will have no trouble with her."

No trouble, Luc had thought with deep satisfaction, would suit him perfectly.

The King had waved his hand, seeming perturbed that they had spoken so long about something he found far beneath his notice. "But enough of that. Let us drink to the future of Miravakia." He had raised his glass.

"To the future of Miravakia," Luc had murmured in response. She would be his wife, and finally, *finally*, he would prove to himself and to the world that he was not cut from the same histrionic cloth as his late parents. Finally he would prove that he, Luc Garnier, was above reproach as well.

"Yes, yes," King Josef had said, and then raised a brow at Luc, as if sharing a confidence. "And to women who know their place."

As she moved closer now, down the cathedral's long aisle, Luc let himself smile, though he did not relax.

She was perfect. He had made sure of it. And now she was his.

Gabrielle could see him now, from beneath her veil, as she finally approached the altar. He stood straight and tall at the front of the cathedral, his gaze seeming to command her even as she walked toward him. Toward their future.

Luc Garnier. Her groom. Gabrielle had never met him—but she had researched him in the months since her father had announced his name. He was descended from centuries of Italian royalty on his mother's side, with a French billionaire father whose fortunes he had doubled before he turned twenty-five. His parents' tumultuous love affair had made headlines while Luc was still young. They had perished in a boating accident when Luc was still in his early twenties, which many claimed was the reason he was so driven, so determined. She fancied she could see his ruthlessness in the line of his jaw, the gleam of his dark eyes.

I can't do this—

But she was doing it.

She had no choice—she had given herself no choice—but she didn't have to watch it happen. She kept her eyes lowered. She didn't want to look at this man—this stranger who would soon be her husband—but she could feel him next to her, above her, as her father handed her off. Luc's large hands took her trembling fingers between his, and guided her the final few steps toward the bishop.

Gabrielle's senses went into overload. Her heart pounded against her ribs while tears of anger and something else, something darker, pooled behind her eyes and threatened to blind her.

He was so masculine, so unyielding. Next to her, his big body seemed to dwarf hers. His body radiated power and menace like heat, surging from their clasped hands through Gabrielle's veins—making her limbs feel dangerously weak.

This is just another panic attack. She ordered herself to breathe. To get a hold of herself and the riot of confusion that made her tremble against the man at her side.

The stranger her father had sold her to.

If Gabrielle closed her eyes she could imagine herself out in the sunshine, basking in the cool winds that swept down from the Alps on the mainland and scrubbed the island clean and cool even at the height of summer. Black pines and red roofs spread across the hilly island, cascading to the rocky beaches that lined the shore. Gabrielle's tiny country was a fiercely independent island in the Adriatic Sea, closer to the rugged Croatian coastline to the east than Italy to the west, and she loved it.

For her country, her father, she would do anything.

Even this.

But she kept her eyes closed and imagined herself anywhere but here.

Anywhere at all…

"Open your eyes," Luc ordered her under his breath, as the wizened bishop performed the ceremony before them. The silly creature had gone stiff next to him, and he could see her eyes squeezed shut beneath her veil—so tight that her mouth puckered slightly.

He felt her start, her delicate hands trembling against his. Her fingers were cold and pale. Her features were indistinct behind the ornate veil, but he could see the fabric move with each breath she took.

"How…?" Her voice was the slightest whisper of sound, but still it tickled his senses. Luc's gaze traveled over the elegant line of her neck, exposed beneath the translucent shimmer of her veil. She was made of fine lines and gentle curves, and he wanted to put his mouth on every one of them.

The rush of desire surprised him. He'd known that she was beautiful, and had anticipated that he would enjoy marital relations with her. But this was something more than *enjoyment*.

He was aware of the tension in her shoulders, the ragged edge to her breathing. He was *aware* of her, and he could hardly see her face through the veil. He felt lust pool in his groin and radiate outward, so that even the touch of her fingers at an altar three feet from the bishop sent heat washing through him.

Then he realized that she was shaking. Perhaps she was not quite as sanguine about this wedding as he'd supposed.

Luc almost laughed. There he was, imagining their wedding night in vivid, languorous detail, while his bride was awash in nerves. He couldn't blame her—he knew that many found him intimidating. Why shouldn't she?

"We will suit each other well," he whispered, trying to sound reassuring. An impulse entirely foreign to him—as alien as the urge to protect her that followed it.

He felt the shiver that snaked through her then, and he squeezed his fingers tighter around hers.

She was his, and he took care of what was his.

Even if he was what had made her nervous in the first place.

Gabrielle forced herself to open her eyes and to take part in her own wedding, even though the stranger's—*her husband's*—voice sent spasms of uneasiness throughout her body. His hand was too hot against hers. He was too close.

Thank God she still had her veil to hide behind.

The bishop intoned the old, sacred words, and Gabrielle had the sensation that everything was moving too fast. It was as if she was both present and far-distant, and out of control either way. She felt Luc's strong hands on hers as he slid the platinum ring onto her finger. She marveled at the size and power of his hand, in contrast to the cool metal she held as she did the same. She heard his voice again when he repeated his vows, this time confident and loud, connecting hard with something deep in her belly.

But nothing could prepare her for the moment when he pulled back her veil, exposing her face to his uncompromising gaze. Gabrielle's mouth went dry. *Fear*, she told herself, though another part of her scoffed at that idea. She could feel him in her pores, surrounding her, claiming her. Something in her wanted it—wanted him—even though he seemed so overwhelming. Even though he was a stranger.

The cathedral fell away. It was as if the two of them stood alone, Gabrielle naked and vulnerable before him. She had known that he was darkly, disturbingly handsome—that women on several continents vied for his attentions. So close, Gabrielle could see why.

His thick dark hair brushed the top of his stiff white collar. The traditional dove-gray morning suit he wore emphasized the breadth of his shoulders and the hard planes of his chest. His features were hewn from stone. There were creases at the corners of his eyes, though she could not imagine this man laughing. He looked harsh, beautiful in the way that the mountains were, and equally remote. His dark gray eyes looked almost black in the light from above, beneath his dark brows. His mouth was set in a firm, flat, resolute line.

He was her husband.

He was a stranger.

More than this, he was a man. And so intensely masculine that Gabrielle could not breathe as he regarded her for a searing moment. As if she was prey and he the dangerous predator. That odd part of her that she'd never felt before thrilled to the idea.

Luc stepped closer, filling Gabrielle's vision. She could smell the hint of his expensive cologne, could see the faint challenge in his gaze. Her lips parted as an unfamiliar sensation coursed through her—something having to do with the accelerated kick of her heart, the disturbing heaviness creeping through her limbs.

One big hand molded to the curve of her cheek. Anchoring her. Holding her. Gabrielle dared not move. She barely breathed. She locked her knees beneath her, suddenly afraid she would topple over.

The heat from his open palm was shocking. It ignited a fire that streaked through her body, confusing her even as something sweet and hot pooled deep inside. Her stomach clenched, and then began to ache. Her breath came in shallow bursts.

Luc did not look away. He tilted her face toward her as he moved even closer, and then he settled his firm mouth against hers.

It was no kiss. It was an act of possession. A hard, hot brand of his ownership.

Luc pulled back, his gaze penetrating, then returned his attention to the bishop—as if Gabrielle had ceased to be of interest to him the moment he'd claimed her.

Gabrielle wanted to scream. She felt the need for it churning inside her, clamoring against the back of her throat.

He was just like her father. He could—and would, she felt certain, in a rush of intuition and fear—dictate her every move. She would be expected to produce heirs. To be naked in front of a man who made her *feel* naked already—even dressed in all her layers of white taffeta, embroidery, pearls.

She could not do this. Why had she agreed to do this? Why had she not said no to her father, as any sane woman would have?

Luc took her hand again, turning Gabrielle to face the congregation. Her attendants moved behind her, moving the great train as the couple began the long walk down the length of the cathedral.

They were man and wife. She was married. Gabrielle's head spun. Luc placed her small hand on his arm and led her down the aisle.

She could feel the power he held tightly leashed in his body as he walked next to her.

Everything inside Gabrielle rose up in protest, making her knees wobble beneath her and her eyes glaze with tears.

This was a terrible mistake.

How could she have let this happen?

CHAPTER TWO

His bride was afraid of him.

"I make you anxious," Luc said in an undertone, his attention trained on her as they stood together in the receiving line after the ceremony.

She smiled, she greeted, she introduced—she was the perfect hostess. And the look she sent him was guarded.

"Of course not," she murmured, smiling, and then turned her attention to one of her cousins, the Baron something-or-other.

Luc expected nothing less from a princess so renowned for her perfect manners, her propriety. Much unlike her royal contemporaries—including the cousin whose hand she clasped now. Luc's mouth twisted as he thought of them, his supposed peers. Paparazzi fodder, like his parents had been—living out their private dramas in full, headline-shrieking view of the voyeuristic world, no matter that it humiliated their only son.

"Congratulations," the cousin said effusively, shaking Luc's hand—his own far too soft and fleshy. Luc eyed him with a distaste he did not bother to hide, and the man's smile toppled from his mouth.

Luc had vowed years ago that he would never live such a useless, empty life. He had vowed that he would never marry until he found a woman as private as he was—as dedicated to not just the appearance of propriety, but of serenity. At nearly forty, he had been waiting a long time.

"Thank you," he said to the Baron with the barest civility. The other man hurried away. Next to him, Luc felt his new wife tense. Perhaps she was not afraid of him, as she'd said. Perhaps it was only a certain wariness. While Luc could not blame her, when grown men quaked before him, it would not do. A healthy respect was one thing, but he did not want her *skittish*.

He gazed at her. Princess Gabrielle was the real deal. More than simply lovely—as he'd thought before—she was beautiful as a princess should be. Her glorious blue-green eyes were said to be the very color of the Adriatic. Standing next to her in her father's *palazzo*, high on the hill overlooking the sea, Luc believed it.

Her masses of honey-blond hair were swept up today, the better to anchor the tiara she wore. Jewels glinted at her ears and throat, emphasizing the long, graceful line of her neck. Her mouth, curved now in the polite smile he suspected she could produce by rote, was soft and full. She was delicate and elegant. And, more than all these things, he knew that she was virtuous as well. She was like a confection in her wedding finery—and she was *his*.

But he had seen the sheen of tears in her eyes back in the cathedral. He had seen the panic, the confusion. Once again, that odd protective urge flared to life within him. He normally did not care whether people respected or feared him, so long as they either did his bidding or got out of his way—but somehow he did not want that reaction from her. She was his wife. And, even though he thought her reaction was more to do with nerves and their new reality as a wedded couple than with any real fear, he felt compelled to reassure her.

"Come," he said, when the last of their guests had moved through the line. Without waiting for her reply, he took her arm and steered her across the marble floor and out to the sweeping veranda that circled the *palazzo*, offering stunning views from the heights of Miravakia's hills to the craggy coastline far below.

"But the meal—" she began. Her voice was musical. Lovely like the rest of her. She did not look at him as she spoke. Instead, she stared at her arm, at the place where his palm wrapped around her elbow, skin to skin.

Luc could see her reaction to his touch in the slight tremor that shook her. He smiled.

"They'll wait for us, I think."

Outside, the ocean breezes swelled around them. Bells rang out in the villages, celebrating them. Their wedding. Their future—the future Luc had worked so hard to make sure he obtained, exactly as he'd pictured it.

But his bride—his *wife*—was still not looking at him. She tilted her chin up and gazed at the sea, as if she could see the Italian coast far off in the distance.

"You must look at me," Luc said. His tone was gentle, but serious.

It took her a long moment, but she complied, biting down on her bottom lip as she did so. Luc felt a stab of desire in his gut. He wanted to lean over and lick that full lip of hers—soothe the bite. But he would take this slowly. Allow her to get used to him.

"See?" His lips curved. "It is not so bad, is it?"

"I am married to a perfect stranger," she said, her gaze wary though her tone was polite.

"I am a stranger today," Luc agreed. "But I won't be tomorrow. Don't worry. I know the transition may be…difficult."

"'Difficult,'" she repeated, and looked away. She let out a small sound that Luc thought was almost a laugh. She smoothed her palms down the front of her gown—a nervous gesture. "I suppose that's one word for it."

"You are afraid of me." It wasn't a question.

When she did not respond, he reached over and took her chin his hand, gently swinging her face toward his. She was several inches shorter than his six feet, and had to tilt her head back to look up at him.

Desire pooled within him, heavy and hot. She was his. From the sparkling tiara on her head, to those wary blue eyes, to the tips of her royal toes. *His.* At last.

"I don't know you well enough to be afraid of you," she told him, her voice barely above a whisper.

His touch obviously distressed her, but Luc couldn't bring himself to let her go. As in the cathedral, every touch sent fire raging through his blood. It had surprised him, but now he found he welcomed it. He stroked the side of her face and ran his thumb across her full lips.

Gabrielle gasped and jerked away from him, her color rising. "I don't know you at all," she managed to say, her voice shaking.

"You are well-known, Your Royal Highness, for always doing your duty, are you not?" he asked.

"I…I try to respect my father's wishes, yes," she said.

Her eyes widened as he gazed down at her.

"I am a man who keeps my promises. That's all you need to know about me today. The rest will come."

She stepped back, and he let her go. He watched, fascinated, as her gaze fell away from his. Yet he could see the flutter of her pulse at her throat, and he knew that she felt the same fire, the same desire he did.

Though he suspected it scared the hell out of her. And that kind of fear Luc could handle.

In fact, he thought, with purely male satisfaction as she turned and headed back toward the reception with only a single, scared look over her shoulder, he looked forward to handling it.

He couldn't wait.

* * *

The wedding meal was torture.

Gabrielle felt as if her skin was alive—she wanted to scratch wildly, to squirm, to tear it off in strips and throw it away. She couldn't sit still in her seat at the high table in the great ballroom. She shifted, desperate to put more space between her body and Luc's right next to her, all the while conscious that they were being watched, observed, commented upon. It wouldn't do to be seen fidgeting in her chair like a child. But she couldn't seem to escape Luc's knowing, confounding gaze, no matter how far away from him she tried to get, and the longer it went on the more agitated she became. He merely watched her, amused.

"What made you decide to get married?" she asked him finally, frantic to divert her attention from the restless agitation that was eating her alive. If the silence continued to stretch between them, *she* might be what snapped.

"I beg your pardon?" he asked.

She was sure that he had heard her. How could he not? Every time she shifted away from him he filled the space she created. His arm, his hard thigh, his shoulder brushed against her. A light pressure here, the faintest brush of his sleeve there. He was crowding her, making it hard for her to take a full breath. She was light-headed.

"Why now?" she asked, determined to break this strange, breathless spell that had her in such a panic. She had never been prone to flights of fancy before—she prided herself on being rational, in fact—but this situation was bringing it out in her. *Which is perfectly normal*, she soothed herself. *Completely rational.* This situation—being married to a perfect stranger like a medieval spoil of war—was what was not normal. Anyone would be beside herself. Though she couldn't help thinking anyone else would have refused to be in this situation in the first place—refused to be married off so cold-bloodedly.

Married. The word echoed in her head, sounding more and more like doom each time. *Married. Married. Married—*

"I was looking for you," he said, in that deep, sure voice of his that sent spirals of reaction arrowing deep into her bones. "The perfect, proper princess. No one else would do."

Gabrielle glanced quickly at him, then away. "Of course," she said politely, to restrain the rising hysteria she was afraid might choke her. "And yet you never met me until today."

"There was no need."

She felt more than saw the arrogant shrug. Temper twined with her distress and she felt her blood pump, hot and angry. *No need?*

"Naturally," she agreed, in the most polite and iciest tone she could manage. "Why meet your bride? How modern of me."

She felt the force of that dark gray gaze and dared herself to meet it. The contact burned. She felt a deep shuddering inside, and had to remind herself to inhale. To blink. To get a hold of herself.

"I am a traditional man," he said. One dark brow rose, challenging her. "Once my mind is made up, that is sufficient." On another man she might have thought there was a hint of a smile at the corner of his hard mouth. But his expression was so forbidding, his eyes so gray. She swallowed.

"I see. You decided it was time to get married, and I fit the bill," she said carefully.

She was like a horse, or a dog—only her bloodline was considered relevant to the proceedings. Had he considered a selection of princesses before deciding she would do? She could feel hysteria rising again, and tried to stave it off by grabbing for her champagne glass. She gulped some of the fizzy liquid before continuing.

"Were there certain requirements to fulfill? A checklist of

some kind?" she asked, her voice rising. But was she really surprised? Men like her husband—like her father—thought the feelings of those around them, *her* feelings, were beneath their notice. Irrelevant.

She thought she might be going mad.

"Gabrielle."

She stilled at the unexpected sound of her name on his lips. Her fingers clenched tight around the delicate stem of her glass, but the way he said her name was like a bell ringing somewhere deep inside her—even though his tone was firm.

She didn't understand it. He hadn't even bothered to meet her before their wedding. And yet he spoke her name and she did his bidding at once, like the purebred dog he thought she was.

"Forgive me," she said crisply, setting her glass down very precisely next to her plate, piled high with food she had yet to touch. "I think the emotion of the day is going to my head."

"Perhaps you should eat," he suggested smoothly, indicating her plate with a nod. Again, the ghost of a smile flirted with his hard mouth. "You must keep up your strength."

Gabrielle's eyes flew to his, then dropped to her plate. He could not mean what she thought he did, could he? Surely he couldn't expect…?

"You look as if you might cry at any moment," he said from beside her, his voice hard as he leaned closer. She could feel the heat of him pressed against the gossamer-thin sleeve of her dress, burning her, and ordered herself not to jerk away. "The guests will imagine you are having second thoughts."

There was no missing the sardonic inflection that time. Gabrielle forced herself to smile prettily for the benefit of whoever might be watching.

"Heaven forbid," she murmured, not realizing she'd spoken aloud until she saw he was watching her, those dark brows raised.

"Eat," he suggested again.

She did not mistake the undercurrent of steel in his voice, and found herself reaching for her fork. Her body obeyed him without thought even as her mind reeled at his arrogance. What if she was not hungry? Would he force-feed her?

She shied away from that thought immediately, afraid to follow it through. He was…too much. Gabrielle took a bite of the fresh-grilled fish on her plate and tried to imagine what life with this man would be like. She tried to imagine an ordinary Tuesday afternoon. A forgettable Saturday morning. But she could not. She could only imagine his dark eyes flashing and his hands strong and demanding on her. She could only picture tangled limbs and his hot skin sliding against hers.

He was too much.

"Please excuse me," she murmured, setting her fork down abruptly and presenting him with her most demure smile—as if her body was not undergoing a full-scale riot even as she spoke. She had to stop it. "I'll be right back."

"Of course," Luc said, in the same polite tone. He rose as she rose, pulling back her chair and summoning one of the hovering servants to aid her with her voluminous skirts, courteous in word and deed. He looked like the perfect gentleman, the perfect husband.

And if she had not seen the knowing gleam in his dark gaze she might have been tempted to believe it herself.

CHAPTER THREE

LUC paid only slight attention to the speech King Josef was making.

"Today Miravakia welcomes its future king," his father-in-law intoned, standing in his full regalia at the head of the long table covered in gleaming silver and white linen, his voice pitched to carry throughout the great room. "But may that day be far off in the future."

Luc was far more interested in his bride at the moment than stale jokes about royal succession, though the guests laughed heartily—as they were expected to do. It was only polite.

Gabrielle, however, did not laugh with the rest. The color was high on her soft cheeks, and she had been sitting far too still beside him since she'd returned from the powder room, her long skirts rustling as she attempted to angle her body away from him. He preferred her attempts at sparring with him, he thought, amused.

"And what about you?" he asked, picking up their conversation from before as if she had not run away in the middle of it. He wondered idly if she believed she'd fooled him—if she believed he was unaware she had made an excuse to escape him. He dismissed the thought. Let her believe it if it made her feel better about her situation.

She threw a cautious look his way, her eyes more blue than green in the dim glow of the ballroom. She vibrated with tension—and, he thought, awareness. Though Luc considered the possibility that she was too innocent to realize it. It seemed impossible in this day and age, but then Luc was used to achieving the impossible. It was one of his chief defining characteristics.

"Me?" she repeated.

"Why did you choose to marry now?" he asked. Once again, he found himself trying to put her at ease, and was amazed at himself. He had stopped trying to charm women when he was little more than a boy. He didn't need it. No matter how he behaved, they adored him and begged for more. But none of them had mattered until this one. For her, he would be charming. Her perfection deserved nothing less.

"Choose?" She echoed him again—and then smiled, though this was not her usual gracious smile, the one that she had been wearing all day, beaming around the room. This one was tighter and aimed at her lap, where she clasped her hands in the folds of her wedding dress. "My father expected me to do my duty. And so I have."

"You are twenty-five." He watched her closely as he spoke, attuned to the way she worried her full lower lip with her teeth. "Other girls your age live in flats with friends from university. They prefer nightlife and the party circuit to marriage or talk of duty."

"I am not other girls," Gabrielle said.

Luc watched, fascinated, as the pulse in the hollow of her neck fluttered wildly. In her lap, her fingers dug into each other. She betrayed no other sign of her agitation.

"My mother died when I was quite young and I was raised to be my father's hostess." She expelled a breath. "I will be Queen. I have responsibilities."

As she spoke, she kept her eyes fixed on her father, who had said something very similar, if Luc recalled correctly. Luc followed her gaze, not at all surprised to see that the King had retaken his seat, without any words specifically directed to his daughter. Evidently this bothered Gabrielle, though she fought to conceal it. Luc could see the sheen of emotion in her eyes, could read her agitation as clearly as if it was in schoolboy Italian.

Luc detested emotion. He loathed the way people blamed their emotions for all manner of sins—as if emotions were separate, ungovernable entities. As if one did not possess a will, a mind.

But Gabrielle, for all the emotion he had sensed in her today, was not letting it rule her. She did not inflict her emotions, her passions, on everyone around her. She did not cause any scenes. She simply sat in her seat, smiling, and handled herself like the queen she would be someday. *His* queen.

Luc approved. He reminded himself that her finer sensibilities were one of the reasons he had chosen her. Her charity and her empathy could not exist in a vacuum. Perhaps emotion was the price.

He decided it was a small one. He decided that he, Luc Garnier, who prided himself on a life lived free of the cloying perfume of emotions, could tolerate hers. Even indulge them on occasion.

"You have made him proud," he told her, nodding at her father, feeling benevolent. "You are the jewel of his kingdom."

Finally she turned her head and met his gaze. The shine of tears was gone, and her sea-colored eyes were clear and grave as she regarded him.

"Some jewels are prized for their sentimental value," she said, her musical voice pitched low, but not low enough to hide the faint tremor in it. "And others for their monetary value."

"You are invaluable," he told her, assuming that would be the end of it. Didn't women love such compliments? He'd never bothered to give them before. But Gabrielle shrugged, her mouth tightening.

"Who is to say what my father values?" she asked, her light tone unconvincing. "I would be the last to know."

"But I know," he said.

"Yes." Again that grave sea-green gaze. "I am invaluable—a jewel without price." She looked away. "And yet somehow contracts were drawn up, a price agreed upon, and here we are."

There was the taint of bitterness to her words. Luc frowned. He should not have indulged her—he regretted the impulse. This was what happened when emotions were given rein. Was she so foolish? How had she imagined the courtship of a royal princess, next in line to her country's throne, would proceed?

"Tell me, Your Royal Highness," he said, leaning close, enjoying the way her eyes widened. Though she did not back away from him. He liked her show of courage, but he wanted to make his point perfectly clear. "What was your expectation? You are not, as you say, other girls. Did you expect to find your king in the online personals? How did you think it would work?"

Her head reared back, and she straightened her already near-perfect posture.

"I… Of course I didn't—"

"Perhaps you thought you should have a gap year from your duties," he continued in the same tone. Low and lethal. "A vacation from the real you, as so many of your royal peers have had—to the delight of the press. Perhaps you could have traveled around the world with a selection of low-born reckless friends? Taken drugs in some dirty club in Berlin? Had anonymous sex on an Argentine beach? Is that how you thought you would best serve your country?"

If he'd thought she was in the grip of emotion before, that had been nothing. Her face was pale now, with hectic color high on her cheeks and in her eyes. Yet again she did not crack or crumble. Someone sitting further away would not have seen the difference in her expression at all.

"I have never done any of those things," she said in a tight, controlled voice. "I have always thought of Miravakia first!"

"Do not speak to me of contracts and prices in this way, as if you are the victim of some subterfuge," he ordered her harshly. "You insult us both."

Her gaze flew to his, and he read the crackling temper there. It intrigued him as much as it annoyed him—but either way he could not allow it. There could be no rebellion, no bitterness, no intrigue in this marriage. There could only be his will and her surrender.

He remembered where they were only because the band chose that moment to begin playing. He sat back in his chair, away from her. *She is not merely a business acquisition*, he told himself, once more grappling with the urge to protect her—safeguard her. *She is not a hotel or a company.*

She was his wife. He could allow her more leeway than he would allow the other things he controlled. At least today.

"No more of this," he said, rising to his feet. She looked at him warily. He extended his hand to her and smiled. He could be charming if he chose. "I believe it is time for me to dance with my wife."

His smile was devastating.

Gabrielle gulped back her reaction to it, suddenly worried that she might scream, or weep, or some appalling combination of the two. Anything to release the pressure building inside her, restless and intense all at once. But that smile—

It changed him. It took stone and forbidding mountain and

softened it, illuminating his features—making him magic. He was, she realized with a delicate shiver of foreboding, a dangerously attractive man.

Dangerous to her, specifically.

For she was helpless before him. He held out his hand and she placed hers within it. Without comment, without thought. Meekly. Obediently. Despite the fact she'd been trying to keep from touching him for hours now. Was she losing her mind?

But she did not dare disobey him. Had anyone ever disobeyed him? And lived to tell the tale?

His smile might have made him momentarily beautiful. His hand was firm around hers, brooking no argument, allowing her no concession as he led her from the high table. The faces of the wedding guests blurred, becoming as indistinct as the flickering candles. She wondered briefly—in a kind of panic—what he would do if she pulled back, tried to move away as she wished. Would he simply tow her along beside him? Or would her body refuse the order and follow his lead without consulting her? She did not think that now—in public, on a dance floor in front of so many onlookers—was the time to test the theory.

He was no playboy, like the few other suitors her father had considered since Gabrielle had reached her majority. This man did not flirt or cajole. There were no pretty words. Only that brief, glorious smile that had jolted through her like an electric shock. Everything else he would demand. Or he would simply take.

He led her to the center of the dance floor. Gabrielle's heavy dress clung to her hips, her legs—made her feel as if she waded through honey. Luc pulled her close, one lean and muscled arm banding around her back, holding her. Caging her.

It had been hard enough to sit next to him throughout the meal. But this—this was agony.

In his arms, there was nowhere to hide. Face-to-face with

him, she felt exposed, vulnerable. Trapped. Her breasts felt heavy and tight against the brocaded bodice of her gown. It took her long, panicked moments to register the fact that she was not having a dizzy spell, that he was moving them around the ballroom with an easy grace and consummate skill, never releasing her from that commanding gray gaze that seemed to see into her very core.

She felt as if she were made of glass and might shatter into pieces at any moment.

"I always wondered what couples talk about," she blurted out, desperate to lessen the tension between them, to divert her attention from that hard mouth now so breathlessly, intimidatingly close to hers, "when they dance at their weddings." She laughed nervously. "But then we are not like most couples, I suppose."

"Again, you forget yourself," he said dismissively, though his gray eyes seemed to darken as she stared up at him. "You are surrounded by a collection of aristocrats, some with ancient family names and kingdoms at their disposal. Do you imagine they are all passionately in love with their politically expedient spouses?"

Infuriating, pompous, *rude* man. How could he speak to her so condescendingly? How could he be her husband?

"I've never thought about it," she flared back at him. "I've hardly had time to adjust to my own 'politically expedient' marriage, much less critique anyone else's!"

His expression did not change, though the arm around her back tightened just a fraction—just enough to make Gabrielle gasp, but not enough to make her miss her step as their dance continued. She was suddenly certain that she did not want to hear whatever he might say next.

"Have you been married before?" she asked hurriedly, hoping to fend him off.

"Never." His brows arched, making him seem both regal and inaccessible at once. Gabrielle swallowed nervously.

"You must have had long-term relationships," she continued. She had no idea what she was saying. "You are forty, are you not?"

"Is this a blind date, Gabrielle?" he asked, his voice dangerously low. "Do you plan to sort out my character through a series of inane questions?"

"I'm trying to get to know you," she replied evenly, raising her chin in defiance. "It seems a reasonable thing to do, under the circumstances. What else should we talk about? The weather?"

"You have the rest of your life to get to know me," he said, with a Gallic sort of shrug. The ultimate dismissal. "Or do you think knowing the way I take my coffee will give you insight? Will it make you more comfortable? The end result is the same. I am your husband."

He was hateful. And his derisive tone ignited the temper she'd worked her whole life to keep under wraps.

"I think you must be the one who is afraid," she declared, anger making her brave. "Why else react so strongly to simple questions?"

She expected him to lash back at her—to try to cow her with his dark gaze or that sharp edge in his voice.

But instead he threw back his head and laughed. It was not long, or loud, but it was real. His gray eyes gleamed almost silver for a moment, and she saw an indentation in his lean jaw—far too masculine to be called a dimple. His eyes crinkled in the corners, and he was once again magical and irresistible.

Suddenly Gabrielle had the sensation that she was standing on a ledge at the edge of some vast cavern, and the ground beneath her feet was shaky. Again that restless tension swelled inside her, terrifying her. Her skin was too small, too sensitive.

He filled her senses. And when he looked down at her again, his expression sobering, she felt something shift inside her. It felt irrevocable. Or possibly insane.

Nerves, she thought, desperately trying to maintain her calm. *Nothing but nerves—and too much champagne on an empty stomach.*

CHAPTER FOUR

ALONE at last in the sumptuous chamber that served as her dressing room, with the reception carrying on below her, Gabrielle stared at herself in the mirror and told herself she was being ridiculous. First, no man could possibly be as intense or overwhelming as Luc Garnier seemed to be. She was letting her imagination run away with her, her emotions heightened by the events of the day. Second, she was forgetting that the tight corset of her dress was probably responsible for her breathless, dizzy reaction to him. He was no magician—able to command her body like some kind of snake charmer. Her gown was simply too uncomfortable—she'd been in it all day.

She had convinced herself, more or less, and started to remove her heavy diamond and pearl earrings when the door opened behind her and he stepped into the room.

Gabrielle froze.

The cathedral and the ballroom had not prepared her—both were so large, so vast. The dressing room was tiny in comparison and Luc seemed to fill it, pushing all the air out the room as he closed the door behind him.

Gabrielle was still unable to move. She stared at him through the mirror as his dark eyes flicked along her spine, then met hers. She felt his gaze like fire, licking into her bones, searing her skin.

"I…" She didn't know what she meant to say, only that she was pleading with him. She put her earrings down on the vanity table in front of her, and twisted around to face him. He had not moved—he still filled the doorway with his rangy, muscled frame—and yet she felt his closeness as if he held her. "I cannot…"

She couldn't say it.

Sex seemed to crowd into the room then, like a thick fog. It was that hot, hard light in his eyes. It was the way he looked at her—as if he owned her, body and soul. It was the parade of images in her head. All of them decadent and disturbing. All of them involving that unyielding mouth of his and those cool, assessing, knowing eyes.

She couldn't bear it.

"Surely you don't…?"

She thought she might burst into tears, but he moved then, and once again she could do nothing but gape at him. He stalked toward her like something wild, untamed. Something fierce and uncompromising came and went across his face, and she knew in a flash that he wanted her—and that she could not survive it.

She could not survive *him*.

"What are you doing?" she asked him, her voice barely a thread of sound, weak to her own ears. He continued toward her, towering above her, forcing her to tilt her head back so she could stare up at him across the great expanse of his rock-hard torso, showed to perfection in his crisp white dress shirt.

Her mind raced. He had said he was traditional—how traditional? Surely he couldn't expect that she would fall into bed with a man she had only met hours before? So what if it was the marital bed?

Could he?

He did not speak. His eyes were shuttered as he gazed down

at her, and then he moved, his big hands catching her around the waist and lifting her to her feet.

He was incredibly, panic-inducingly strong. Gabrielle's world tilted and whirled, and then she was in his arms again—but this time they were not on a dance floor, surrounded by witnesses. This time they were all alone, and he pulled her much too close, until she sprawled against him, her breasts flattened against the wall of his chest. They ached. Gabrielle moaned—whether in protest or terror, she did not know.

"I will not attempt to claim any marital rights tonight, if that's what you're afraid of," he said then, his breath fanning over her face.

"I… Thank you…" Gabrielle said formally, and was then furious with herself. As if it was *his* decision to make! As if *she* did not exist!

"We will grow into each other, you and I," he told her. His mouth was so close, and it both tempted and terrified her in equal measure. She remembered the feel of his mouth against hers in the cathedral. Brutal. Territorial. She didn't know why it made her knees tremble and her core melt.

"But our wedding night should be commemorated, should it not?" he asked.

"I don't—"

But he wasn't really asking.

His mouth came down on hers, as uncompromising and hard as she remembered—as he had been since she'd met him so few hours before. This time he tasted her lips only briefly, before moving across her jaw, her temple, learning the shape of her. His mouth was hot. Gabrielle felt her own fall open in shock—in response. She felt feverish. Outside herself.

Something in her thrilled to it—to him—even as the rest of her balked at such a naked display of ownership. Her hands flew to his shoulders, though it was like pushing against stone.

Then, as suddenly, he set her away from him, a very masculine triumph written across his face.

"You are mine," he said. Claiming her. He reached over and smoothed an errant strand of her hair back into place, the tenderness of the gesture at odds with the harshness of his words, his expression. "Change into your traveling clothes and meet me outside the ballroom, Gabrielle. We will stay on the other side of the island tonight." He paused. "Wife."

She stood frozen in place for a long time after he left. The air rushed back into the room with his departure. Her heartbeat slowly returned to normal. Her hands eventually stopped shaking.

But inside her a new resolve hardened, and turned into steel.

She could not survive him, she had thought in a moment of panic. But she was not panicked now, and she knew that it was true. It was not simply that Luc Garnier was another man like her single-minded father—though she knew that he was. It was not even that he clearly wanted things entirely his own way—what man in his position, having bartered for a royal wife and his own eventual kingdom, would not? It was that she was so detestably weak.

Weakness had led her here, to this sham of a wedding night. She was married to a man who terrified her on a fundamental level and she had walked calmly to her own slaughter. Her father had not had to coerce her—he had only announced his intentions and Gabrielle had acquiesced, as she always did, because she'd thought that somehow her doing so would impress him. Instead, it had only made him less inclined to consider her feelings at all.

What a thing to realize now—far too late.

Gabrielle blew out a shaky breath and knew, on some level, that acquiescing to Luc Garnier would be far more damaging and permanent. She would not survive it intact—not as the Gabrielle she was now. She could not handle his heat or his darkness—and she would not be recognizable to herself if she tried. She would go mad—lose her mind.

She thought of his fierce gaze, his resolute expression, and felt as if she already had.

She had never stood up for herself. She had let her father order her around her entire life. Now her husband would do the same. Worse. He would demand even more from her. Suddenly Gabrielle could see her life stretch out before her— one decision made by her husband after another until she ceased to exist. Until she was completely absorbed into him, lost in him. A man like Luc Garnier would accept nothing less than her complete surrender.

She took a deep breath, then released it. She looked around the chamber as if she'd never seen it before. Perhaps she had simply never realized until now that it was a prison cell.

And it was past time to escape.

Luc's body shouted at him to turn around, return to the dressing room and finish what he'd started.

He was hard, ready. His blood was pumping and it had nearly killed him to take his hands off of her soft skin.

Her taste was addictive. Sweet, with an underlying kick.

He paused in the long corridor outside her door. He wanted to bury himself in her—in his wife—and make them both delirious with need and release. Again and again until they were exhausted from it. It was a complication he hadn't foreseen— and he had been so sure he'd covered all the angles.

Tonight he could allow himself some amusement on that score. It was not very often that Luc Garnier was taken by surprise. He had expected to desire her—she was a beautiful woman and he had long had a taste for classic beauty. Who did not? But the need raking through him and tempting him to charge back through the door and claim what was his—that was unexpected.

Perhaps it was not a complication. Perhaps it was merely a side benefit—confirmation that he'd made the correct choice. The fact that he knew very few men in his position who lusted after their wives meant nothing. When had Luc been at all like other men?

He forced himself to walk away from her door, to leave her in peace. For tonight, at least.

They had their whole lives to explore this combustible chemistry. He could allow her one night to come to terms with it.

His mouth curved at the idea of behaving benevolently—for any reason. It was a new sensation, and not entirely pleasant. He was not a man who denied his appetites.

But it was only for tonight.

In the morning he would continue her education. He would touch her until she welcomed it, until she begged him for more.

And then all bets were off.

It had been so easy, Gabrielle marveled almost a week later, looking out over the endless sea of lights below her. Los Angeles gleamed and beckoned, sprawled out before her, seeming seductive and immense from Gabrielle's spot high in the Hollywood Hills.

Gabrielle couldn't believe *how* easy it had been—it made her wonder why she had waited so long to do something simply because she wanted to do it, without worrying about the feelings or opinions or wishes of anyone else.

Gabrielle had left the *palazzo* after a quick change of clothes, driven down to the docks, boarded a ferry—and been in Italy by morning. Once she'd made her way to Rome she had booked herself into a hotel for the night and called an old friend from university. Cassandra had not missed a beat, despite the fact she and Gabrielle had not seen each other in ages. She had apologized for the fact that she could not be in California to greet Gabrielle because she was filming in Vancouver, but she had offered Gabrielle the use of her house. Gabrielle had boarded a flight the next morning, had a brief stopover in London, and had been in Los Angeles by early afternoon.

Not bad for an obedient princess who had never lifted a finger in protest her whole adult life.

Tonight Gabrielle stood out on Cassandra's deck and sipped at a glass of white wine. Hollywood was splayed out before her, sparkling into the warm night, the lights and sounds wafting up from the famous Sunset Strip far below. She loved California—what little she'd seen of it in her jet-lagged and emotional haze. She loved the eucalyptus and rosemary-scented hills, with columns of cyprus trees scattered here and there. She loved the coyote howls at night and the warm sun during the day. She loved the red-topped houses that reminded her of home, and the hints of the Mediterranean throughout the landscape—houses clinging to the hilltops in clusters and the sea far below.

Gabrielle felt rebellious: American. She had helped herself to her friend's closet, as Cassandra had urged her to do. She wore denim jeans and a silk blouse tonight, and had left her feet bare. She curled her toes into the sun-bleached wood beneath her and reveled in the freedom of even so small an action. Her hair swirled around her shoulders in the warm night air. The outfit was light years away from the way she dressed normally—the pathologically proper Princess wore Chanel suits in soothing pastels and kept her hair in a smooth French twist.

And Gabrielle never wore jeans. Never. Her father believed jeans were "common," and out of deference to him Gabrielle hadn't worn a pair since her days at university. Tonight she decided she loved them. She liked the feel of the denim against her skin, defining every inch of her thighs and smoothing down her calves to tease her toes. They felt decadent and disobedient—two things Gabrielle wanted very much to be herself.

How had she let this happen? she wondered again, as despair moved through her body like a wave. How had she allowed her life to get so far from her own control? How had she *handed* it to someone else with so little thought? She balked at the idea that she would go so far to please someone—but facts were facts. She *had* handed over her life. First to her father, and then to her brand-new, terrifying stranger of a husband.

Behind her, the doorbell echoed through the pretty California Craftsman house, built like an expanded bungalow. Gabrielle smiled. That would be the housekeeper—the efficient and helpful Uma, who had promised to return with groceries for Gabrielle so she need not venture out into the hair-raising traffic on the Los Angeles streets.

Gabrielle padded to the front door, her bare feet making the faintest whisper of sound against the dark wood floor.

"You're a lifesaver—" she began, throwing the door open.

But it was not Uma who stood there.

It was Luc.

CHAPTER FIVE

Luc. Her husband. On the doorstep in front of her.

A kind of fire exploded through Gabrielle's body, heating her skin and raising the fine hairs on the back of her neck. Her mouth went dry.

If she could have moved she would have run for it, bare feet and all—she would have scrabbled up the hillside and run until she collapsed. Anything to put space between them.

But she was paralyzed by the fury in his dark gaze, the rigid set of his muscular shoulders, the power emanating from his strong frame. He was no less imposing in a cotton sweater and dark trousers than he had been in a morning suit on their wedding day.

In fact, the ferocious masculinity he trumpeted from every pore was even more intense than she remembered—with the California night behind him, and that hot banked rage she could practically taste simmering in his nearly black gaze.

She had been wary of him a week ago. But she could see—instantly—that the Luc Garnier she had met on her wedding day had been tame and sweet next to the one who now stood, incensed, on the doorstep before her.

You should have kept running, a little voice inside her insisted. *You should never have stopped.*

"Hello, Gabrielle." His voice was rich, dark and mocking. Gabrielle flinched. "I think you forgot something in your haste to get away," he continued, looming over her on the front step.

His shoulders blocked out everything else—or perhaps it only seemed that way through the tears of reaction she fought to hold back.

"I—forgot something…?" she stammered.

His mouth twisted. "Your husband."

And then Luc walked inside, ignoring the wineglass that fell from her bloodless fingers, stepping over the shattered glass and the pool of liquid that spread across the floor—and never once taking his eyes off of her.

How dared she stare at him like that? When she had humiliated him on their wedding day—and run off across the planet! After all the leeway he had granted her—a mistake he would never make again.

How could he have been so wrong? How could he have mistaken her character like this? If one of his subordinates had been responsible for an error of this magnitude Luc would have fired and destroyed him. Had he only believed what he'd wanted to believe? Had he succumbed to the lie of her charms like any other, lesser man?

Luc bit back the bellow of rage and betrayal that threatened to spill out. He would remain in control. He would not sink to her level. Though it cost him, and he felt himself snarl with the effort of controlling his temper.

His eyes raked over her—his recalcitrant princess. Not perfect at all, but a lie. A lie who was now his wife.

Tonight she did not look like the obedient, biddable Princess Gabrielle he had chosen so carefully. It was as if that woman did not exist. *That woman had never existed!* Her thick tresses flowed around her, free and wild and the color of honey. She smelled sweet and fresh, like the scent of jasmine outside, rising up from the hills. And she pulled away from him as he stepped over the threshold and closed the door behind him— closing them inside.

Her feet were bare. Tight blue jeans showcased the curve of her hips and the long, slender length of her legs. Luc imagined those legs wrapped around his neck and felt himself harden immediately. He wanted her.

He hated that he wanted her. When she had played him for a fool. When she had managed to deceive him—he who prided himself on his immunity to such deceptions. He should never have believed the lie of her wide eyes, her trembling lips. Her supposed charity. Her proclaimed innocence. Moreover, he should have claimed what was his immediately, and to hell with her feelings.

So much for his urge to protect her. He would never indulge it again.

"What are you doing here?" Gabrielle asked into the tense silence, her eyes huge, as if she could read his mind.

She backed away as he approached, keeping a good two strides between them. She danced backward into the living room, and then moved to the back of the nearest sofa—as if a piece of furniture would provide a barrier. As if she would need some kind of barrier.

Luc might have found her amusing in other circumstances. But not much had amused him since he'd realized that she'd not only abandoned him, but had done so at a moment calculated to cause the most gossip, the most speculation. He thought he might hate her for that. He stopped in the center of the room and crossed his arms over his chest, to keep himself from doing anything he might regret.

"What am I doing here?" He smiled without humor. "I couldn't allow my bride to spend our honeymoon alone, could I?"

"Honeymoon?" She shook her head. "I don't understand."

"What did you think I would tell them, Gabrielle?" Luc asked softly. "Did you consider it at all? What exactly did you think of as you abandoned me in the middle of our wedding reception, surrounded by our guests?"

"I'm sorry," she said, almost helplessly.

She clasped her hands in front of her. Perhaps she did not know that the movement pushed her breasts forward, drawing his attention to them and creating an intriguing shadow beneath her blouse. But he suspected she did. He suspected that everything about her was calculated.

And he'd fallen for it. Hook, line and sinker. He who had never lost control with a woman in his life, who had gone to such lengths to prevent exactly this scenario, had been well and truly played. He took a step closer.

"Sorry?" he repeated. He kept his tone mild. "That's all you have to say?"

"I...I had to leave," she said, that musical voice low. Pleading. "I can't do this—don't you see?"

He did not see. He felt. A churning mess of sex, fury, bitterness and possession that flared whenever he thought of her and was like wildfire now that she was in the same room. Even though he hated what she was—what she'd done to him. Because of it, perhaps.

"Why don't you tell me?" he said, moving toward the fireplace. He leaned casually against the mantel, though he did not feel in the least bit casual tonight. "I see my wife. The woman I married in a cathedral packed full of most of Europe. Tell me what you see that I do not."

"You're a stranger!" Frustration made her voice shake. Color was high on her cheeks, accentuating her classic bone structure and the perfection of her full mouth. "You... I met you at the altar!"

"So?" He straightened from the mantel. "This is your objection? This caused you to race across the world to get away from me?"

"Are you insane?" She let out a short laugh. "We don't live in the Middle Ages. Normal people get to know each other before they get married."

"But you and I are not normal people," Luc said, with an edge in his voice, closing the distance between them. Hadn't they already discussed this? Was she truly so naïve? He somehow doubted it after the past week. He watched as she fought against her urge to run from him as he rounded the couch. It was written across her face. Yet she stood firm. "You are the Crown Princess of Miravakia."

She held her hands out, warding him off.

"This is my fault," she said desperately.

"Then we agree," he bit out.

"I should have objected sooner," she continued, wary. "I've spent the days since the wedding asking myself how I could have let things get so far. My only excuse is I…I am not used to denying my father's wishes."

"Yes," Luc said bitterly. "The obedient, demure Princess Gabrielle, of whom I have heard so much. It was first assumed that you were kidnapped, you understand. Because no one could imagine the biddable, dependable Princess disappearing in such a public, humiliating way *deliberately*."

She flinched. "I am so sorry." Her eyes searched his. "You must believe me! I didn't know what else to do."

"You are my wife, Gabrielle." His voice was cold. Bitter. "That means something to me even if it does not mean anything to you."

Her color deepened. "I can't tell you—"

"And let me make something clear." He reached over and took her upper arms in his hands, forcing her to stand still, to look up at him.

Her skin was like satin. He wanted to strip her clothes from her body and explore it. He wanted to punish her. Or both at the same time. He should have done it from the start. He should have taken her in that dressing room of hers, with her wedding dress still on. He should never have played at the courteous gentleman—a role he knew nothing about and never would.

"Please—" she started.

"I do not believe in bloodless faked marriages of convenience," he told her with finality. "It will not happen with us."

"What? What do you mean?" She blinked. "There must be—"

"I mean exactly what I said." He drew her closer, so that her panicked breath caused her firm breasts to brush against his chest. "You made vows. I expect you to honor those vows in word and deed. Do I make myself clear?"

"But—but—" Gabrielle shook her head, trying to clear it. But Luc was so close—his hands burning into her flesh. She couldn't seem to catch a breath. "You can't be serious! We don't even know each other!"

"I think I've gotten to know you well enough over the past week," he said, his voice almost tender, at odds with the darkness in his eyes, the hard set of his jaw. "As I chased you across the planet, the scorned and humiliated husband you abandoned so cavalierly. What more do I need to know?"

"No!" She was trembling, her eyes glazed with frustration or fear, but he no longer believed her. Or cared. "I didn't— I never—"

"Tell me, Gabrielle—when did you decide to deceive me? Or was this your plan all along?" His voice was harsh. So close, his hard features seemed made of stone.

"Of course not!" she cried. "Why can't you understand? I made a mistake!"

"Yes," he hissed. "You did."

Something sparked then, in the dark depths of his gaze—something hot and wild, bitter and lethal.

She knew what he was going to do in the split second before he did it—and she thought she screamed. She thought she cast him away from her with the force of that scream. But she didn't make a sound. She didn't move at all.

His merciless mouth came down on hers and she was lost.

Luc's mouth was hard—and inexpressibly delicious. Gabrielle's head fell back as her mind spun out, leaving her dizzy and weak. He held her jaw in his strong hand—guiding her lips with his.

He did not seduce, caress. He took. He demanded. He possessed.

And Gabrielle's body burst into flame after flame of sensation. It was as if her body spoke to his in its own ancient language, and Gabrielle could neither control it nor understand it. She felt hot, and then cold. Luc deepened the kiss, playing with her tongue, her lips. Her hands crept up to the warm soft cotton of his sweater, then pressed against the planes of his chest. He made a slight sound of encouragement, or passion, as his powerful arm wrapped around her hips and dragged her up against the length of his body.

She could feel him from head to toe, pressed hard against her, imprinting himself, his taste, into her senses.

She was insane with the feel of him—the glory and the terror.

"Kiss me back, damn you," he growled, breaking away for only a moment.

Gabrielle stared at him, dazed. And then once again his mouth took hers, slanting to get a better, sweeter fit, and Gabrielle ached. Her breasts ached as she pressed against the implacable strength of his chest. Her belly ached, and she pulsed with heat between her legs.

Gabrielle felt the glass of the sliding door behind her, the coolness sharp against her overheated skin. She hadn't noticed that Luc had backed her into the door until he pressed her back against the glass. He moved his fingers into her hair, fisting his hand in the silky mass.

Once again he pulled his mouth away from hers. His face seemed harsh, dangerous. Gabrielle shivered. His dark eyes bored into her, and she had the irrational thought that he could *see* what his kisses had done to her—could see the almost painful throbbing low in her belly, in the molten core of her.

She opened her mouth to speak—perhaps to beg him to take her, to ease her agony, to let her go. She would never know.

The doorbell rang again, echoing through the house.

Luc glared. "Are you expecting someone? Is that why you ran to California—to meet your lover?"

"My…" Gabrielle shook her head, reeling. She couldn't make sense of his words, or the suspicion that glittered in his dark eyes. "It's the housekeeper," she said, her voice no more than a whisper, and huskier than it should have been. She looked down and saw that her hands had curled into fists. "She's come to bring groceries."

Her voice trailed away into nothing. She looked up, and the full force of his angry gaze slammed into her.

His eyes glittered. "There will be no more lies, Gabrielle. No more betrayal. Do you understand me?"

"Yes," she said, although she had no idea what he was talking about. But he was so elemental, so terrifying. How could she say anything else?

You are weak, she told herself bitterly. *And he is your greatest weakness of all.*

"Somehow," he said softly, though nothing else about him gentled at all, "I don't believe you." His hard mouth twisted. "Wait here."

CHAPTER SIX

THANK God for this distraction, Gabrielle thought in a daze, sinking gratefully into the leather couch.

She could hear Luc's low, commanding voice from the kitchen, and Uma's happy chatter in return, but what she noticed most of all was Luc's absence.

Breathing room. Space. As if the room had expanded when he left it.

Her lips still trembled, her knees felt suspiciously weak, and she could *taste* him in her mouth. A rich wine against her tongue, sending out little thrills of response through her limbs. She could feel his hard body against her skin as if he was still touching her. As if she wished he was still touching her. As if he had marked her, somehow.

Gabrielle couldn't seem to stop the riot in her mind, the chaotic surge of emotions and impressions that flooded through her veins and left her feeling electrified. Altered. Scared. And dangerously, absurdly excited.

How could she respond like that? How could she find him so intoxicating that even his anger couldn't dissuade her? Her body didn't care if he was angry, if he overwhelmed her, if his expressions or his words were cruel.

Her body craved his touch. Even now. Still.

Gabrielle blinked and gazed down at herself, as if she was looking at a stranger. She had never spent much time thinking about her body. She knew that she was considered beautiful, of course; her father had insisted upon it, demanded she tend to her beauty as she tended to any other royal duty. She was to be beautiful, but never flashy. Hers was a quiet sort of beauty that lent itself to charitable work and her role as her father's hostess, and her thoughts about her appearance tended to focus entirely on how best to utilize it.

Tonight, however, she felt vivid. Alive. Wild and untamed. Not quiet or capable, but loud and crazy with need. How had he done that? How had he turned her body against itself without so much as asking her permission?

He would not ask. She knew that on some elemental level. He would not ask for what he could take. He would simply take it—as if it was his due.

She inhaled sharply against the riot of images that conjured up.

And then her eyes clapped to his—as if she'd sensed him there in the wide archway, watching her with that impenetrable gray gaze. As if she'd summoned him.

She felt a tickle along the nape of her neck and wondered almost helplessly if he had some kind of beacon, something that emanated from him and announced his presence. Shouted it before he entered the room.

Behind him, the front door slammed shut.

They were alone. Again.

Gabrielle felt her mouth run dry. She ran her palms along her thighs, trying to settle herself. She felt jittery beneath her own hands—silly with a need she only half understood.

"So quiet," Luc said, his dark voice mocking.

Gabrielle didn't know if it was defiance or fear, but she felt something move through her then. She knew it was related to the feeling that had compelled her to leave the palace—to escape. This time it brought an angry flush to her cheeks as she tossed her head back.

"What's the point in speaking if you continue to cut me off?" she asked, for all the world as if she felt as bold and careless as he seemed to be. She eyed him. "You're quite rude, you know."

She was startled by the flash of his teeth and the sound of his sudden laughter. That same dent in his jaw glinted for a moment—the one that had mesmerized her on their wedding day. It fascinated her anew.

She hadn't meant to amuse him. Had she? But she felt a warmth course through her anyway, suggesting that some part of her wanted to please him, to amuse him. Maybe more of her than she wanted to admit.

Why should she want to please this man, when he had done nothing but scare and overwhelm her? What did that say about the kind of person she was?

But had she ever been anyone else?

Once again, she despaired of her own weakness.

"I am rude, yes," Luc agreed, closing the distance between them with sure strides. "And ruthless. And arrogant. And whatever else you need to call me. Does it make you feel better to say it out loud?"

"Better?" Now it was Gabrielle's turn to laugh, as if he wasn't bearing down on her with so much barely leashed, alarming purpose. "Why would it make me feel better to find myself shackled to such a man?"

"Shackled." His dark eyes gleamed as he stopped before her, forcing her to crane her head back, looking up the long, solid length of his spectacular body—the one she had now felt crushed against her own, from her neck to her calves. "Now, there's an idea."

Gabrielle felt her lips part as the vision he'd intended

rushed at her. Her arms bound. Her naked flesh open and inviting, and Luc so dark and powerful above her. She shivered. His mouth flattened.

"An idea you like, I think. Somehow I am not surprised."

"I…I don't know what you mean."

But she lied. And he knew it.

He reached down and took her hand into his bigger one. She did not resist as he pulled her to her feet—she couldn't seem to summon the will to do anything but stare at him. She thought of her hands bound, tied against the four-poster bed in the master bedroom that she'd been sleeping in so restlessly. Their bodies writhing together. Once again she was paralyzed. Was it fear, she thought, or something else?

Longing, something more honest whispered in the back of her mind.

She thought he would kiss her again when he brought her in close—near enough to feel the heat of his body, to smell the scent of his skin.

But instead he traced unknowable shapes across her cheek and down to her collarbone, tested the length of one thick strand of her hair, and then stepped back.

"Put on your shoes," he ordered her, curt and sure. "We're going out."

"Out?" Was that her voice? So breathy and insubstantial? Why did he turn her brain to cotton and fire?

"To dinner," he clarified and then smirked, as if she were simple.

"Dinner," she repeated, and was furious with herself when his smirk sharpened. She was not usually so stupid and dull-witted—yet from the moment she'd met him, from almost their first words, she had done nothing to show him that she was anything else. What must he think? That her father had sold off his idiot daughter?

"Surely the concept cannot alarm you?" Luc said, in that intensely sardonic tone. "I feel certain you must have had dinner before."

Sarcasm. How delightful.

"Not with you," she snapped at him. "And not in this city. But, yes, thank you—I have had dinner before. How good of you to point it out to me." He was not the only one who could be sarcastic, she thought defiantly. But he ignored it.

"How interesting that you would choose to run away to a place you know nothing about."

She couldn't help but notice that he didn't look interested at all. He looked furious.

"I came here because my friend lives here," Gabrielle said, with a helpless sort of gesture around Cassandra's living room, ignoring the words *run away*. It was harder to ignore the dark look he had trained on her. "I knew I would be safe here."

"Safety is relative, Gabrielle," Luc murmured, his gaze almost feral. "And transient."

She eased away from him, feeling the sofa at the backs of her knees. She edged her way along its length—away from him.

She was all too aware that he had let her go.

"Happily, there are any number of excellent restaurants in this city," Luc told her, as if they were discussing nothing more than dinner plans. "And several that suit my purposes completely."

"I'm surprised you want to go out in public," she shot at him—emboldened by the distance she'd put between them. Whole strides and a glass table. "You'll have to behave, you know. No browbeating or threats in front of witnesses."

She was pleased with her own daring—so uncharacteristic—and she couldn't regret the words once they left her mouth, despite the way Luc's brows snapped together. But then, impossibly, he let out another laugh.

"Look at you," he said, that deep voice turning to silk. "So proud of yourself for standing up to me. Do you know *why* we're going out, Gabrielle?"

"Because you're hungry, I imagine." She sniffed, as if it was of no matter to her.

"Because your little stunt has resulted in our being splashed across every European tabloid imaginable," Luc corrected her, still in that almost soft tone.

The hair rose on her arms and her neck, and she understood on a deep, physical level that he was more furious than she'd seen him. That she was in more danger from this Luc than the louder, more obviously angry Luc she'd seen before.

"'Luc's Luck Runs Out.' 'Runaway Princess Bride.'" His hands clenched at his sides convulsively as his eyes bored into her. "You have made me the laughingstock of Europe."

"I…" She didn't know what to say, or why she felt the strangest urge to go to him, to try and soothe him. "I'm sorry," she said. "The tabloids have never paid any attention to me before. I never gave them a thought."

"Clearly." He let out a derisive sound. "But now, my darling bride, you will think of nothing else. You will smile and make eyes at me, do everything in your power to convince the world that we are nothing but a couple in love—do you understand?"

"I'm not an actress—" she began, frowning.

"Are you not?" His words cut into her, delivered with so much irony—so much disbelief.

What must he think of her? She blinked away the sudden heat across her face, behind her eyes. One of her hands flew to her throat, where she could feel the agitation in her pulse as well as her skin. She realized what she must look like and forced the hand back to her side.

"I don't see the purpose of this." Gabrielle took another step back, trying to ward off the unexpected pain. Why should she care if he thought ill of her? It only proved how little they knew each other. And yet…

"You do not have to see the purpose of it," he told her. "You need only to put on your shoes—and suitable trousers. My tastes do not run to barefoot brides cavorting in vulgar displays for the world to see. You will be Queen one day. I remember this, even if you do not."

"We cannot pretend that this marriage is anything but a farce, bare feet or not," Gabrielle protested, stung by his words. "Why would you want to parade it in front of cameras?"

"Listen carefully," he ordered her, closing the distance between them with such dizzying speed that Gabrielle gasped, faced with the unwelcome knowledge that he'd been toying with her. *Letting her* think she was getting the space from him she so desperately wanted.

He reached over and took her head between his hands, forcing her to be still, to look at him. Holding her suspended in his grasp.

It should not have made that mad heat punch into life in her belly. But it did. She felt ashamed of herself. And as if she'd been set on sweet, deadly fire.

"This marriage is no farce," he whispered, his mouth too close, his eyes burning with dark fury. "This marriage is real. I do not believe in divorce, even from deceivers like you. We do not have to like each other. But you have made this relationship into a matter of public scorn and ridicule and I will not have it. I will not allow it."

"I've never deceived you!" Gabrielle felt her eyes swim, whether from hurt or desire she was afraid to discover. Her lungs felt constricted, contained, as if he held them between his powerful hands as well.

"Everything about you is a lie," Luc gritted out. But his hands were gentle—holding her, not hurting her. He bit off an oath. "Especially this," he muttered thickly, and took her mouth with his.

Once again that piercing pleasure, all fire and need. Once again the roar of response charged through her. Gabrielle felt her nipples harden even while she shuddered and her body readied itself for him. She forgot to breathe, to think, as his lips demanded her response and then took it, again and again.

He set her away from him, his gaze shuttered. Gabrielle felt weak. Loose. Dangerously softened. Her hand moved to her lips, as if she could still feel the mark of him—his possession.

"Gabrielle." He said her name as if he hated the sound of it, but then his cruel mouth twitched into something not quite a smile. "Put on your shoes."

CHAPTER SEVEN

LUC watched Gabrielle closely from across the small table at the famous Ivy restaurant in Beverly Hills, drumming his fingers against the white linen tabletop. He tried to keep his temper under control, but he could feel it bubbling up, threatening to erupt.

He could not allow that. Not in a place he had chosen because it was so public, so exposed. He kept a lid on his fury.

Barely.

She had done as he asked. She'd smiled for the scrum of photographers who camped out in front of the Los Angeles landmark, and had even laughed with every indication of delight when Luc had kissed her in a shower of flashbulbs.

So calculated, he thought now. Though another part of him argued that she had only done what he'd told her to do.

Now she sat facing him, her mysterious calm smile locked across her mouth, looking as if she was having a marvelous time trying to pick out celebrities from the crowd around them on the outdoor patio.

He found it infuriating.

He wanted to mess up her perfection, wreck that serene countenance—see what boiled underneath all that bland politeness. Because he'd already had a taste of it, and it had sent a dark need raging through his blood.

"It appears you are quite an actress after all," he said, pitching his voice low enough to reach her ears but go no further. He watched her stiffen, though her smile did not falter. Just as she'd done at their wedding reception, she managed to avoid broadcasting even the slightest hint of any internal discomfort.

"If you mean that I know how to behave in public, then, yes, I am," she said. Her voice was smooth, though her chin rose slightly in challenge. "I always assumed that was a result of good breeding."

"The same good breeding that inspired you to abandon your own wedding reception?" he asked smoothly. "How proud your father was of *that* display."

He could see her response in the quiver of her lips and the tense stillness of her body—but, even so, to the untrained eye she might have been discussing the perfect California night that held them both in its soft, warm cocoon.

"That was an aberration," she said. Through her teeth.

"Lucky me."

"Tell me," she invited him, leaning close so he could see the storm in her sea-colored eyes, which pleased him more than it should have, "what would you have done in my position?"

"I would have honored my promises," he replied at once, harshly.

"How easy for you to say." She took a ragged breath. "How easy for you to criticize something you know nothing about."

"Then tell me about it," he suggested, sitting back in his chair. "We have an entire dinner to get through, Gabrielle, and then the rest of our lives. If there is something you feel I should know, you have all the time in the world to explain it to me. Who knows?" He smiled slightly. Coolly. "I might even see your point of view."

"You will never see my point of view," she snapped back at

him, surprising him. "You have no interest in why I left—you only care that it injured your pride. Your image! What explanation could possibly soothe the wounded pride of a powerful man?"

Luc definitely did not care for the sarcastic tone she used. But he watched her until she glanced away, one hand moving to her throat.

"You will never know unless you try," he said. Daring her.

"My father has had very specific expectations of me ever since I was a girl," she told him after a moment. Reluctantly. "He was—is—a hard man to please, but I tried. I got only top marks at university. I bowed to his wishes and became active on the charity circuit, supporting the causes he thought best instead of using my degree to help him run our country. He did not want his Crown Princess involved in matters of state unless it was to plan events or throw parties. Whatever he wished, I did."

"Go on," he urged when she paused again. He tried to picture a young, motherless Gabrielle, growing up in the shadow of her grim, humorless father, and found he did not like the image he conjured up. He wasn't sure he believed it, either. Surely the obedient child she described would not have run off the way she had?

"It's not such an interesting story, really," she said, refolding the napkin on her lap. "I tried my best to please my father up until the day he married me off to a man I'd never met without so much as asking me my opinion on the match." Her shoulders squared. She looked at him, bravely, and then away. "I felt as if the world was closing in on me. Trapping me. I didn't mean to leave you like that—but I had to go or be swallowed whole."

"And you couldn't speak to me about it." He tried to keep his voice light, but she glanced at him nervously and he knew he'd failed. "You couldn't ask for my help."

"Ask for your help?" She looked mystified by the very idea. She actually let out a startled laugh. "I wouldn't…" She shook her head. "You were a stranger," she said, frowning. "How could I explain this to you when it wasn't personal at all, and yet involved you all the same?"

Part of him wanted to rage at her—to demand that she acknowledge that she should have run *to* him, not *from* him—but he clamped down on it. Why was he so quick to believe this story? Poor little lost princess, desperate to please her autocratic father. It was the story of every rich, entitled noble he'd ever met in one form or another, and yet somehow Gabrielle had found a way to splash them both across a thousand glossy tabloids—something no other woman had managed in a very long time. She claimed it had been unconsciously done on her part—he thought it far more likely a deliberate act. Her first chance for a full-scale rebellion, for all the world to see. Maybe the perfect princess had indeed chafed against her role—but not in the way she claimed tonight. Perhaps the tabloids had been the best weapon she could come up with, and he the best victim.

"I am your husband," he said, as mildly as he could, his gaze trained on her face. "It is my duty to protect you."

"Even from yourself?" she asked wryly.

He did not respond—he only watched her reach for her wineglass, tracking the slight tremor in her hand. She pressed the glass to her lips. Luc wondered how he could find such a simple gesture so erotic when he wasn't sure a single word she spoke was the truth. She was a liar—she had deceived him and made a mockery of him in front of the world—and still he wanted her.

He wanted her—needed her—with a fury he could neither explain nor deny. It had started as he'd watched her smile her way through a week in Nice, had simmered as she'd walked toward him down the aisle in Miravakia, and had only been stoked to an inferno in her absence. Now that he had tracked her down she was so close to him—just across the tiny table—and he burned.

"I am no threat to you," he told her, though he knew he made himself a liar as he said it. He didn't care.

Her eyes met his, large and knowing across the table.

"You'll forgive me, I think," she said, with that same wry twist of her mouth, turning his own words back on him, "if somehow I cannot quite believe you."

The dinner passed in a strange, tense bubble. Gabrielle was aware of far too much—the scrape of her blouse against her overheated skin, the swell of her breasts against the silky material of her bra, the rush of warm, fragrant air into her lungs, and always Luc's inflexible, brooding presence that she was convinced she could *feel*. He was too big for the table—he overwhelmed it, his long legs brushing up against hers at odd, shocking intervals, his body seeming to block out the night. She could see, taste, only Luc. She barely touched her plate of grilled shrimp, and was startled when the waiter brought them both coffee.

"You don't care for coffee?" Luc asked, in that smooth voice that sounded so polite and yet set off every alarm in her body.

She kept herself from squirming in her seat only with the most iron control.

"What makes you say that?" she asked, stalling. She picked up her cup and blew on the hot liquid, wishing she could cool herself as easily.

"You made a face," he said. "Or I should say you *almost* made a face? You are, of course, too well trained to make one in public."

"I don't think I did anything of the kind," she said stiffly, aware that he was toying with her, yet unable to do anything but respond as he intended. It made her feel annoyed at herself. As if she was a mouse too close to the claws of a cat.

"I am beginning to understand the intricacies of your public face," he told her, eyeing her over his own coffee. His gaze was neither kind nor cutting, but it made Gabrielle shiver slightly. She decided to blame the slight breeze. "Soon enough I will be able to read you, and what will you do then?"

"If you could read me," she replied lightly, "you would not have to wonder if I was lying to you."

"There is that."

"Then I hope you're a quick study," she threw at him, riding the wave of emotion that flashed through her.

"Oh, I am," he promised her, his dark voice hinting at things she was sure she didn't want to understand. Their eyes met and her breath caught—and then his gaze traveled over her mouth, pointedly.

Gabrielle swallowed and put her coffee down.

"Are you finished?" he nearly purred, raising a hand to signal the waiter. He never looked away from her face. "We can head home whenever you like."

Head home? she repeated to herself. *Together?*

That was impossible. Surely he didn't expect…?

"Home?" she echoed nervously. "You mean Cassandra's house?"

"Is that her name?" He sounded bored. And also amused.

"Surely you have a hotel somewhere?" she said.

His lips twitched. "I own a number of hotels," he said. "Most of them in Asia—though there are a few in France and Italy as well. None in this country."

"That's not what I mean," she said crossly. "You can't stay at Cassandra's house with—with—" She cut herself off. Flustered.

"With you?" He finished for her, his gaze enigmatic. "Can't I?"

"Of course not. That's ridiculous. We are not…" She looked down at her lap and saw her hands had curled into fists. Resolutely, she unclenched them both and placed them before her on the table, like a civilized person. "And you can't think that we—"

"I meant what I said earlier," Luc said—so unbending, so resolute. His gaze serious. "I expect you to be my wife—in every sense of the term."

"You're insane!" she whispered, too overwrought to scream as she wanted to do. Though she felt the force of it as if she had made enough noise to tear at her throat. Or perhaps that was the other part of her—the part that was fascinated by him? The part that secretly wanted to be his wife, *in every sense of the term*, just as he'd said. She drew in a jagged breath.

"Tell yourself whatever you need to tell yourself, Gabrielle," he threw back at her, his dark eyes glittering. He leaned forward, seeming to loom over the table, dwarfing her before him. "You play the offended innocent so well, but you're fooling no one."

"I have no idea what you're talking about," she blustered, with all the bravado she could summon.

"All I have to do is touch you," Luc murmured, reaching over and capturing her hand with his. He laced his fingers with hers—the contact shocking, intimate. Flesh against flesh. Electricity leapt between them, igniting her blood—making her gasp. Her breasts felt heavy, and once more she felt that hot, wet need between her legs.

His dark eyes shone with a hard, masculine triumph.

"And again," he said quietly, with an intense satisfaction that she couldn't mistake, "you are made a liar."

Outside the restaurant, Gabrielle fought for composure while Luc called for his driver.

She wanted to rage at Luc—for his high-handedness, for his ruthlessness, but most of all because she feared that he knew things about her body, about *her*, that she was afraid to discover.

She knew she could not survive this. Him. No matter how loudly her body clamored, no matter the searing ache radiating out from her core. He would change her, mark her. She couldn't let it happen—and yet, as he had proved, all he had to do was lay his fingers against hers and her body betrayed her in an instant.

She was desperate.

But she had to keep her plastic, perfect smile on her face, no matter what. She had to act delighted when Luc returned to her side, and she had to gaze at him adoringly as they waited for the car. All of which she executed flawlessly, as if she really was the carefree new bride he wanted her to be.

What would it be like if I was that blissful new bride? a traitorous voice whispered. If she had not run—if she had stayed with him that evening—where would they be now?

Gabrielle shook the disturbing questions away, and concentrated on maintaining her composure. Luc accused her of being an actress, as if it was something shameful, but he was lucky she'd had the training she'd had. Without it she might have shattered into pieces right there on the street and left it to the photographers to clean up the mess.

"Finally," Luc said, much closer than she'd expected, as his sleek black car approached the curb.

His lips barely touched the delicate shell of her ear, and yet she felt the hot lash of desire spike in her belly and then flood through her body. She hated that he affected her this way. She hated that her knees weakened at the thought of the night to come, even when her mind balked.

There would be no *night to come*. She barely knew the man!

She'd been in his company for all of six hours in total—including their wedding! He was delusional if he thought she would leap into bed with him—no matter if he was, technically, her husband. No matter if her own body seemed to want him in ways she was afraid to explore.

She knew that she would be burned without recognition—forever altered—if he got his way, and she could not allow it to happen. She had to hold on to what little sense of self she'd somehow wrested from the ruins of the last week—from her whole previous life as a dutiful, controlled princess. It was as if she'd finally woken up from a very long bad dream, and here was a nightmare in human form, threatening to suck her back down under.

But she kept her smile firmly in place as Luc handed her into the backseat of the luxurious sedan. She opened her mouth to thank him, but his attention was caught by one of the men standing in the pack of photographers jostling for position around the car.

Luc stiffened almost imperceptibly, and the harsh curve of his mouth went glacial. It was frightening to watch—though Gabrielle allowed herself a quick moment of relief that he was not looking at *her* that way. As if he would like to tear the man apart with his bare hands, and was strongly considering doing so.

"Silvio—what a delightful surprise," Luc said in deeply sardonic Italian. "What brings you to California? A vacation?"

However angry he had been with her—and was still—Gabrielle knew he had never used that horribly cold, vicious tone before. Not on her. Not yet. She shivered. The other man, obviously a paparazzo if the camera slung across his neck was any indication, seemed oblivious. He even smiled at Luc, a bland and casual smile that drew attention to his cold eyes, as if he could not sense the danger.

"Where my prince goes, I follow," he replied in the same language, his mockery all too evident. "How's married life treating you, Luc? Is it all you dreamed now that you've finally run her to ground?"

"And more," Luc said, baring his teeth. "I'm sure I'll see you around."

"You can count on it," Silvio shot back.

"I always do," Luc retorted, that feral smile in place.

Then, much worse, he climbed into the car next to Gabrielle, closed the door, and turned all that icy ferocity on her.

CHAPTER EIGHT

LUC was silent as the sleek car hugged the twists and turns that led up into the hills—but it was a kind of silence that was much worse, Gabrielle thought with mounting trepidation, than anything he might have said.

She could *feel* him. Without looking at him—because she didn't dare—she could sense the way he lounged against the butter-soft leather seat, his indolent posture at odds with the dark power that seemed to hum through him like a live wire. She could feel anger come off of him in waves, like heat. The way his dark eyes consumed her sent terrified shivers down her spine. He seemed to fill the entire car with his presence—crowding her, pressing against her, cornering her—though he was not touching her at all.

How could he do such a thing? How could he seem to possess her without so much as lifting a finger?

She called her reaction terror, but some deep feminine knowledge inside her knew better and whispered the truth. Her breasts felt swollen, surging against the confines of her bra, her blouse. Her breath came too fast, too shallow. Her legs felt restless, and a kind of panic made her want to squirm, to run, to scream. It clawed at her throat and teased at her eyes, and she didn't know what she would do if the pressure grew stronger. Would she burst? Explode?

The car pulled up in front of Cassandra's house, and Gabrielle stared at the pretty Craftsman façade—though she did not see it. She was aware only of his quiet, brooding presence behind her as she stepped from the car. She could feel only her own body's panicked response in the staccato beat of her heart, the heat that suffused her, and the tell-tale dampness between her legs.

How could this be happening? When he seemed so angry— so furious with her? Had she no self-respect at all?

But then she already knew that she did not—could not have. A woman with self-respect would surely not have found herself married to a stranger. She would not have married him, and if she had she would not have abandoned him at their wedding, only to be pursued across the world like some runaway bride. Whether she called it weakness or a lack of self-respect, it worked out to the same thing in the end—didn't it?

"Come," Luc said, taking her hand with his in a dictatorial gesture that pulled her closer to his body—too close. His dark gaze seemed to glitter in the dark night, and his mouth pulled into a merciless line. "It is time to stop playing these games."

She did not exactly *run*. She opened the door and then hurried away from him. Luc watched her move with a quiet satisfaction, knowing she walked far too quickly for someone unaffected.

He knew better. He'd seen the high color on that gorgeous face of hers. He'd watched her growing agitation on the drive home.

Seeing Silvio—that gutter-swine—had only solidified the rage he'd been carrying around ever since the humiliating moment he'd realized that his perfect, proper princess had in fact *done a runner* and left him to face the consequences of her choices. Silvio was the worst of the paparazzi who had hounded

Luc for years. And he'd been after a story like this for ages—ever since Luc had lost his temper in what seemed now like another life, and blackened the lowlife's eyes at his parents' funeral.

That had been the last time Luc had been splashed across so many tabloids—the last time he'd excited so much scandalous comment. Since then there had been the odd photograph, depending on who he happened to be dating, and the usual complaint that he was "notoriously reclusive." When in truth he simply did not wish to fund Silvio's parasitic existence.

Damn Gabrielle for playing right into Silvio's hands. Damn his *wife* for giving scum like Silvio ammunition.

But Luc knew exactly how to make her pay.

His gaze lingered on the sway of her hips, the twitch of her hair against her shapely back. He smiled—hard.

He was looking forward to it.

Inside the house, Gabrielle fled across the living room and found herself face-to-face with her reflection in the sliding doors. She placed her palms against the cool glass, surprised when her hands didn't sizzle with all the heat she was sure she was letting off.

Luc did not turn on the lights when he came in behind her. A streetlight from outside spilled into the room, lengthening the shadows he stalked through, as quiet and as dangerous as some lethal jungle cat.

She was his prey. She could feel it in a primal way, down into her bones.

"There is nowhere left to run, Gabrielle." His voice was so low. Menacing. It seemed to vibrate against her spine, sending waves of reaction radiating out and consuming her.

"I'm not running," she said, tilting her chin up. She hated how childish she sounded. So pointlessly defiant. He laughed. It sent a new chill through her.

"You should have known how this would end," he contin-ued, as if she hadn't spoken. "You should have known better."

"I don't know you at all," she said—but it came out as little more than a whisper.

And it was a lie. She knew things she would prefer to ignore. Her body knew him better than she wanted to admit—and it cried out for him in the darkened room, no matter how she longed to deny it.

"You are mine." Possession and finality rang in his voice.

"You do not own me," she breathed at him, bracing herself against the glass door and straightening her back against him. "No one can *own* another person!"

"Does it make you feel safer to think so?" he asked, mocking her. "Do you think political correctness will help you tonight?"

She didn't know what she thought—she only knew he was too close, and every cell in her body screamed at her to flee. To do anything and everything she could to escape what was coming as surely as day followed night. To hold on to herself—because he would raze her to ashes in his wake, and who knew what she might be when he was finished?

Luc stopped behind her. His hands came up to hold her shoulders. He traced the shape of her arms beneath his palms. The reflection in the glass blurred his features slightly—made him seem more approachable, somehow, less remote.

Or maybe it was the way he touched her that made her blood sing his name, and washed away any half-formed thoughts she might have had left of escaping him.

She felt the warmth of his skin through the thin fabric of her blouse. She felt the surprising hardness of his palms as they moved along the lines of her body.

As if he was testing her. Training her. The thought made her belly clench.

She shuddered, and felt herself weaken. She who was

already so weak where he was concerned. A delicious, terrifying languor stole through her, moving like fire in the wake of his hands, daring her to ease back against the hard, solid length of his body, as if she could no longer hold her head high of her own volition. She felt him against every inch of her back—too hot to the touch.

She should say something. She should remind him that they were strangers. She should try to put him off somehow. It was too soon—it would always be too soon. She should refuse to do whatever it was he was planning to do—was already doing.

She knew that there would be no turning back.

But she couldn't seem to move.

He used his mouth then—heat and breath against her temple, her neck, the fine bones and hollows near her collarbone.

She had the impression of fire—flames licking from his mouth to ravage her body—and then he was turning her to face him, tilting her head back. She saw his dark and troubled gaze before his mouth fastened to hers, and then she could think of nothing but the way he kissed her.

She was lost. Again and again and again.

His mouth plundered hers, taking control and molding her mouth to his will. This time Gabrielle knew how to kiss him back, but she could do little more than that as he took her mouth with the same ruthlessness as he'd done everything else.

It was as if a storm raged through her—crushing and incinerating everything in its path. Gabrielle felt the power and strength of his mouth against hers, and everything else was part of the inferno that swept through her. Fire. Awe. Panic.

She pulled away from him—wanting to wrench herself out of his arms, but managing only to put the barest breath of space between them.

She would be lost forever if she let this happen. Something

powerful and old inside her had been telling her this since she'd laid eyes on him, and she could feel the truth of it resonate through her, sending aftershocks through her skin, her blood, her mind. Her lips burned. And—most treacherous of all—she yearned for him. For more.

She searched his dark eyes, his implacable face, but found only stone. Iron.

She felt dizzy, suddenly—overwhelmed. He was so remote, too powerful, and she knew that she could not emerge from this the same as she was now. He would alter her, change her, forever marking her life into *before* and *after*—and she was terrified that *after* would mean the end of her, of who she was, of who she wanted to be. He would reduce her, dominate her, and she had no idea what would become of her. Gabrielle felt her lips part on a half-formed protest, or perhaps a plea—anything to stop the storm that was Luc Garnier, anything to put more space between what remained hers and what he would take.

But he stopped her with another kiss, this one even more frightening for all it was gentle. Gabrielle felt herself shake against him.

"Enough," he said quietly against her mouth. "The time for talking is over."

She went straight to his head, far more potent than any alcohol he'd ever tasted.

Luc kissed her again and again, bending her backward over his arm, holding her firmly against him so he could roam freely across her mouth, her neck. She tasted like nothing he had ever imagined before—sweet, addictive, and so hot it burned to touch her. It burned worse when he stopped.

She kissed like an innocent. Like the lies she'd told.

Tasting her, Luc wanted to believe every last one of them.

He groaned and swung her around, pulling her down with

him onto the sofa and settling her across his lap, her knees on either side of him. He sucked in a breath as their hips made contact. He surged against her softness and made her moan in response.

Luc's hands roamed over the curves he'd longed to possess since he'd first laid eyes on her. He pressed his open mouth against her neck, and thrilled to hear the low keening sound she made in the back of her throat. Impatient to see more of her, he pulled the silky blouse over her head, baring her breasts to his view.

"Please…" she said, her voice deep and husky, cascading over him. With a single, sure motion, Luc released the clasp of her bra and tossed the filmy piece of lingerie aside.

Her breasts jutted before him, firm and proud, her nipples standing to attention at eye level. He could no more resist taking one tender bud into his mouth than he could resist his next breath. He covered the other breast with his hand, testing her shape, learning her curves.

Braced above him, trapped between his hardness and the heat of his mouth, Gabrielle swayed in his arms. Her thick, luxuriant hair fell around them in wild waves, smelling of flowers and musk, cocooning them together.

When her moans grew throaty, Luc switched his mouth to the other nipple, laving the tight peak with his tongue while his hand explored the breast he'd left behind.

"Luc—" She gasped out his name and he liked it. He liked the desperation in her tone, the blind need on her face.

She was his. He would never let her forget it again.

"Please," she cried. "I don't—I don't know—"

He sucked her nipple into his mouth, hard, moved his hips against hers, and she exploded in his arms.

Her head fell back, exposing her throat as the shudders racked her slender body. Triumph and a dark, keening sort of need ignited Luc's blood. He wanted to be inside her. He wanted to personally investigate every last lie her trim body with its surprising lushness wanted to tell. He wanted to explore them all, with his mouth hot against her and himself deep within her, until the only truth she knew was him.

She lifted her head as if it was far too heavy, and blinked at him, dazed.

The worst part was that he no longer cared what she was lying about, how she had deceived him. As long as he could touch her, he didn't care about a damned thing.

It made him mean.

"Are you always so responsive?" he asked acidly. "Or is this a show for my benefit?"

She shook her head slightly, a faraway look on her lovely face and then a slight frown between her eyes. She shifted position, still straddling him, and Luc bit back a groan as the movement ground her harder against him.

"Why would I put on a show for you?" she asked.

"Touché," he muttered, and claimed her mouth once more.

Only as he explored her mouth, wondering if he would ever get used to the kick of it, did it occur to him that she had sounded bewildered instead of spiteful.

He thrust the thought aside.

He had to get inside this woman—his wife—or go insane. *Now.*

CHAPTER NINE

GABRIELLE had to be dreaming.

She could almost convince herself of it—a foreign country, a strange house, the compelling and dangerous man who held her in his strong arms and reduced her to a shivering wreck. Aftershocks still skated along her limbs, so much concentrated pleasure making the air feel heavy around her. But Luc's skin was warm next to hers, his kisses drugging and irresistible.

She knew she was awake—more awake, perhaps, than she had ever been before.

"Luc…" She tested his name, tested whether or not she was dreaming.

"Hush." His mouth came down on hers, a tidal wave of sensation crashing over her. If she could have gasped or screamed—but he was everywhere, crowding her and holding her, molding her body to his.

He swept her up into his arms then, breaking from another scorching kiss to haul her tight against his hard chest. He rose from the sofa in a single, effortless movement, not trumpeting his lean, whipcord strength but using it without thought—which made it that much more shocking. Breathtaking. Gabrielle felt a flutter of reaction steal through her. His dark eyes gleamed in the shadows, her throat felt dry, and she worried that she had lost the ability to speak.

She could only stare at the uncompromising planes of his face as he moved through the house, holding her in this parody of lovers on a wedding night. The wedding night she had run away from. Would he have carried her this way a week ago, in the dressing room of her father's *palazzo*? Or later that night, in the suite of rooms he'd reserved across the island? Would she have felt this same way, as if she was under his spell, enchanted, helpless to look away from him for even a moment? She could remember too well how commanding and overbearing he had seemed in his morning coat—his shoulders so broad, his torso so lean and muscled, his eyes a darker gray than his coat. He was even more disconcerting tonight, bothering her, *troubling* her in every sense of the word. A deep shudder moved through her then, starting deep inside and working its way out. She was afraid. So deeply afraid.

But Gabrielle had to be honest with herself, and the truth was stripped bare and evident as she looked at him, caught in his gaze as surely as a fly in a spiderweb. She felt the steel bands of his strong arms hold her easily—the heat of him soaking into her, surrounding her, while leftover pleasure still hummed through her body.

It was not fear that warmed her blood, that made her feel so feverish and out of control. It was not fear that made her crave more of his hot mouth, his clever tongue, his masterful hands.

It was desire.

Gabrielle might not have felt it before—not like this—but she knew what it was. She knew what the ache between her thighs meant. What the tightness of her nipples meant. She thought she knew exactly what it all meant, and even while it terrified her she could admit that something in her thrilled to the battery of new sensation. Welcomed it. Wanted it.

The same old doubts and fears crowded into her head then, louder and more insistent. She blinked and closed her eyes against him, as if that could block him out, even as she clung to him—even as he moved with that same inexorable force through Cassandra's home.

She did not know this man. This marriage was a horrible mistake, foisted upon her by her father. She had spent twenty-five years in blind obedience, but she was blind no longer, and she knew without a shadow of a doubt that marriage to Luc Garnier would destroy whatever burgeoning independence she'd discovered in the short week since she'd found the courage to stand up for herself.

He would take her over completely, and it started here. It had already started—the moment he'd appeared at the door. She would disappear into him, drown completely.

It was already happening—every time he touched her.

"Luc—" she said again, pulling back from him, suddenly aware of how helpless she was, held high against his chest this way. How clearly it underscored his power and her lack of it. Never in a lifetime of powerlessness had she seen it so starkly, so clearly.

His eyes gleamed, and then everything tilted wildly. Gabrielle gasped even as she registered that he'd tossed her onto the wide four-poster bed in the master bedroom as if she weighed no more than a feather. She bounced once, and then his hard body sprawled across hers, pinning her to the mattress. Gabrielle froze, while her heart beat wildly within her chest.

Sensation fed into sensation—his hands roamed from her hips to her shoulders, then around her waist to test the shape of her bottom and trace the indentation of her spine—until Gabrielle could hardly tell the difference between them. There was only this fire, this need. He was heavy and hard all over. He crushed her into the mattress, pinning her, stealing the breath from her body…and she gloried in it. She felt electrified from each point of contact, from the dark addiction that was his clever, cruel mouth against hers, from the wall of his chest above her, from the hard muscled thigh that pressed intimately against her own. Her breasts throbbed and she felt herself melt, hot and wet beneath him. Her body was ready for him—ready and desperate and *now*.

He braced himself on his hands, and Gabrielle fumbled with the buttons on his shirt, the material as soft as a cloud beneath her fingers. She had to put her hands on his skin—to see if she was the only one feverish with this need, to see if she could feel the same relentless desire in him. Muttering a curse, he twisted until he could rip the shirt from his torso, then tossed it to the floor. And then there was nothing between her breasts and his muscles, hard-packed beneath his tight, smooth flesh. Only her skin against his skin.

The delicious slide of it, the textures and the feel of so much strength so close against her, made her mouth go dry.

Her hands trembled as she ran them across the fascinating planes of his chest, through the dusting of dark hair between his hard pectoral muscles and arrowing down his taut abdomen, the differences between them making her shiver and want. She throbbed everywhere. She could feel her pulse pound in her head, her heart and between her legs. Remembering the joy of it when he'd done it to her, she leaned closer and placed her open mouth on the tight male nipple she discovered. He groaned, and she turned her attention to the other nipple.

"No more," he muttered in Italian, dark and gruff into the crook of her neck.

The same place on his body tasted of salt and something else—something that reminded her of Cypress trees and Adriatic breezes.

"Do not tease me."

With deft, sure hands, he stripped the rest of his clothes from his body, and then did the same for Gabrielle, lifting her hips as if she weighed no more than one of the down pillows she lay against, pulling off her trousers with ruthless efficiency.

Then he laid his naked body against hers, making Gabrielle gasp. She felt the crisp hair on his thighs press against her own smoother ones. His hard chest rubbed deliciously against her nipples. She could feel his erection strain against her softness, making her dizzy with want. Need. *Luc.*

He braced himself on his hands above her, and looked down at her. The frank hunger in his gaze excited her almost more than she could bear.

She felt wanton. Powerful.

"Don't tease me," she whispered, daring to throw his own words back at him.

His mouth curved, but it was less a smile than something purely male and sexual. It connected with something deep inside Gabrielle and made her ache.

Everywhere.

"Your wish is my command, Your Royal Highness," he murmured.

And then, without any warning, he twisted his hips and thrust into her.

He came up hard against her, hearing her cry out as he did so. It was so unexpected—so surprising—that Luc stopped moving, his breath scraping in and out of his chest as he stared down at her in shock.

"You are a virgin." It was not a question.

Her eyes swam with surprised tears as she looked up at him, her small hands braced against his chest as if holding him off.

"You should have told me—" But he cut himself off. She

had told him in every way she could. Her wariness of him, though she had looked at him with such sensual curiosity at their wedding reception. Her artless kisses. The innocence he had first wanted to honor, and then had cynically believed she was faking. When exactly should she have explained that she was an untouched virgin? When he was having a temper tantrum over that piece of filth paparazzo? He hadn't wanted to believe the evidence before him.

But he hadn't meant to hurt her.

"Yes," she said after a moment, squirming against him. He thought she was trying to get away from him, little realizing that her movements had quite the opposite effect. He was deep inside her, all the way to the hilt, and yet she kept wriggling, drawing him in even further. It was torture. Sweet, delicious torture.

"Of course I'm a virgin!" Again she moved restlessly, crossly, beneath him. "What does it matter?"

He searched her face. She was flushed as much from anger as passion, but he knew her body now. He knew how she responded. He moved experimentally, just a roll of his hips, and she gasped again, the color on her cheeks deepening. Confusion washed across her face, and she bit down on her full lower lip.

"Did that hurt?" he asked quietly. He did it again, and her breath came out in a rush.

"I…I don't know…" she stammered, her gaze almost troubled.

"I would not have hurt you if I'd known," he told her. He traced the curve of her neck with his fingertips, down to her perfect breasts. Regret seared into him, and he kissed one proud crest, then the other. An apology of sorts.

"If you'd known…?" she repeated. She blinked. "Because you thought…?" She didn't finish the sentence, but stared up at him in sudden outrage. Her hands balled up into fists against his chest.

"Yes, I *thought*." He rolled his hips again, pleased to see her outrage fade into a tiny sigh, her hands unclenching and sliding down toward his hips. "You are not fresh from the convent. I did not negotiate our marriage with your Mother Superior. You are a grown woman."

He did not say *I thought you were a liar.*

He felt her softness and her heat surround him. She cradled him between her thighs.

"No," she said, her voice breathy, "I was not in a convent. Not technically. But of course there was no… I could never—" She broke off, her cheeks turning a deep shade of rose.

Inside his chest, something stirred to life and expanded, triumphant.

Mine, he thought. He wanted to roar it. No other man had ever touched her. No other man ever would. She was his. More completely than before.

"For all intents and purposes you might as well have been in a convent," he murmured. "I understand."

He exulted in it.

"Luc…"

His name on her lips excited him. He kissed her deeply. He moved against her slowly, carefully. Deliberately.

"Trust me," he whispered, sinking deep into her, sheathing himself completely in her hot depths.

He built the fire with long, slow kisses. He fanned each and every flame that he could think of, kissing the elegant line of her neck, reaching around to hold her bottom on the shelf of his hands. He set an easy, unhurried pace—encouraging her to do more than simply accept his thrusts. Soon she moved to meet him, her hips rising of their own accord, as if she couldn't help herself. Her legs moved restlessly, then found their way to rest on the back of his. His hands caressed her and guided her, reaching between them and stroking her in her most sensitive place until her breath came in short, hot pants and her head thrashed from side to side against the pillows.

Mine, he thought.

When she flew apart, he followed.

A long time later, Gabrielle woke with a start.

At first she didn't know what could have woken her. But then, almost immediately, she recognized Luc's hard body against her own, sprawling across the bed with one arm carelessly thrown out over her. Had that been what pulled her from sleep? She had never shared a bed with someone else before. It felt strange and almost invasive to have so much big male animal crowding into her space, taking up so much real estate on the mattress that had seemed vast to her before. Tonight it seemed woefully inadequate. He was so *large*.

The events of the long night teased at her, vivid images chasing each other through her head, each one connected to sensations she could still feel in her limbs. She felt used in a way she never had before. She felt like a woman. As if she had finally discovered the purpose of her breasts, her hips. As if she'd been created to give him pleasure, and as if she should glory in it.

Gabrielle looked at Luc as he slept, his firm, cruel mouth soft and almost sweet in slumber, making him appear much more approachable. Younger and smoother. She smiled to herself. It wasn't that he looked boyish—she couldn't imagine Luc as a boy; the harsh lines of his face forbade it somehow—but he seemed so much *less* in sleep. More easily contained, maybe. Less frightening. Less overwhelming. Not so edgy and abrasive. Easier, somehow, to contend with.

She shivered, though she was not cold, and turned, so her back faced him and she could stare into the darkness. Was she changed, as she'd feared? Altered forever? How could she tell?

She hadn't expected it to be so...*physical*. She hadn't expected to feel him so deep inside her body, or that having someone invade her in that way would make her feel so small and yet so strong all at the same time. It was so confusing even now. She had known the mechanics of the act, of course, but the execution had been so...*Luc*.

He was like a force of nature. He had hurt her, and then he had made her feel nearly wrung out from the pleasure he could give her. Even now, wide awake and tormenting herself in the night with questions she wasn't sure she wanted answered, she wanted *him*. His very nearness made her nervous—made her body hum in yearning, even though she could feel aches in various places from new and unusual activity. Even after everything that had already happened she wanted him. Was that more of her abominable weakness? Or was he simply that powerful?

"You are thinking so loudly that no one can sleep," Luc said then, making her flinch away from him in surprise. When she turned over to face him he was watching her, those dark eyes bottomless in the dark of the bedroom.

"I'm sorry," she said automatically. Then wondered why she should apologize for something so ridiculous as his claim that he could hear her *thinking*. He was not supernatural. No matter how he might appear sometimes. "You must be a very light sleeper."

He reached over and traced the frown between her eyes, smoothing it away with his strong fingers. She leaned into his touch the way plants leaned toward the sun, and with as little conscious thought.

"You do not need to worry," he told her in that commanding voice. "I will take care of you."

It sounded like a vow. All his rage from earlier in the evening seemed to have left him. All that ferocity and anger. Though he was no less imposing a figure, lying there so dark and masculine against the sheets, his well-sculpted shoulders broad enough to block out the rest of the room from her view. Gabrielle discovered she was holding her breath and let it go—only to catch it again when his fingers moved to drag across her lips in an unmistakably sensual gesture.

But, "Sleep," he said.

"I don't know what woke me," she whispered. She felt that speaking in her normal voice would be like talking too loudly in a church. She could sense that a great storm had passed in him—the one that had taken them both over, the one she was still not certain she had survived intact—but she didn't know why. She was afraid to upset the delicate balance that seemed to hover between them. She wanted his eyes to remain so clear and very nearly soft as he looked at her—she wanted his mouth to curve as it did now.

She didn't know why she should want any of those things. Was this what she had feared? Was this how the losing of herself began? Or had it already started—was it already too late?

In the dark room, so late at night, Gabrielle wasn't sure she cared.

"Perhaps I have created a monster," he said, sliding one strong hand around to cup the back of her neck and draw her close to kiss her. "Perhaps you can only rest for a short amount of time before you require me again."

Was he teasing her? In a good-natured way? Gabrielle found this possibility shocking—but no more shocking than her body's immediate response to the feel of his mouth against hers. Her nipples hardened, and she felt herself soften for him. On command. At the slightest touch. Even the faint soreness between her legs failed to keep the desire from coiling in her middle. She slid her hands into his thick black hair, reveling in the texture of it, the shape of his head, his hard body once again moving over hers, crushing her so deliciously beneath him.

But she only whispered, "Perhaps," and lost herself in him once again.

CHAPTER TEN

WHEN Gabrielle woke again, late morning sunshine spilled
into the room, disorienting her as she sat up in the big bed.

She knew immediately that Luc was gone—from the bed,
from the room—knew even before she looked around to
confirm it. His presence was too elemental, too disturbing—
she knew she would have sensed it if he was near.

Gabrielle pushed the heavy mass of her hair back from her
face, stretched, and took a moment to catalog the various twinges
and aches in interesting places in her body. She felt herself flush
as she remembered all the ways she'd moved, all the things she'd
done, all the things he'd taught her in one short night.

Not that she had been a prude, exactly, before this strange
marriage. She might not have done as much with the opposite
sex as her contemporaries had. Or, truthfully, anything at all. Her
knowledge of men might have been more theoretical than practical. But she'd dreamed, and her dreams had never been particularly tame. She had assumed her imagination filled in the blanks
adequately enough. But she had dreamed about sex the way
she'd dreamed about love—all so vague and hidden in soft focus.

Nothing about Luc Garnier was in soft focus. He was vivid
and challenging and shockingly physical.

Gabrielle swung out of bed and pulled on the silk robe she'd left draped over the plush armchair near the dark mahogany armoire. She tiptoed over to the bedroom door. It was open a crack, and she stood near it, straining to hear. From far off she heard the unmistakable deep tones of Luc's voice. She eased the door shut and realized that her breathing had gone shallow—her flush deepened and spread. What had he done to her? And how could she possibly face him now, knowing what it had been like between them in the dark—in the bed?

Pressing her hands against her cheeks, as if that could calm her, Gabrielle turned and headed for the *en suite* master bathroom. She was, apparently, no longer able to control herself, but she could certainly control how she looked. Best not to appear before him half-naked and wanton, with her hair in disarray. Gabrielle might not have known what to do about the intimidating man who had suddenly become so intimate with her, but she certainly knew how to dress herself to hide her emotional state. It was one of her gifts.

After a shower—which she knew she drew out longer than she should have, so anxious was she about this morning after— Gabrielle blew her hair dry and then took care to dress like the princess she was. Not the Americanized version of herself Luc had been so displeased with the day before.

She chose a pair of cream-colored linen trousers made especially for her by the Miravakian designer she had hired to oversee her official wardrobe, and paired them with a whisper-soft cashmere sweater in a champagne hue. Then she arranged her hair into its usual French twist, smooth and elegant. She added the slightest dab of scent behind each ear, and put on a pair of pearl studs that announced their pedigree—and hers— with an understated gleam. She chose her makeup with care, deciding that Luc was the kind of man who, like her father, preferred the fantasy of the bare face—little realizing the amount of work and skill it took to produce such a look. But understated elegance was what Gabrielle was known for and what Luc had signed on for—the pinnacle of her personal achievement to date, she thought then, her mouth twisting into a wry smile.

Casting her thoughts aside, since they did her no good, Gabrielle eyed herself critically in the full-length mirror on the back of the closet door. She would do. Gone was last night's wild creature, with her uninhibited hair and bare feet. In her place was the Princess Gabrielle she had always been. Muted. Pastel. *Soothing.*

It was her armor.

Luc looked up when she walked out through the sliding glass doors onto the deck, where he was taking one in a series of business calls that had started early in the morning. He murmured a few closing remarks in French, then ordered his assistants to fax him the relevant documents before hanging up and giving his wife his full attention.

The bright California sunshine spilled over her, highlighting the fine elegance of her features. She looked every inch the well-bred, well-behaved Miravakian princess he had originally believed her to be—from the smooth hair swept back from her face to the quietly sophisticated apparel. This woman standing before him was the one he'd seen in Nice—not a hair out of place, oozing composure.

She nodded at him, her cultivated social smile at the ready. "I'm sorry that I slept so long this morning," she said. "I hope I haven't kept you waiting."

So polite. As if she had not spent a long, sweaty night in his arms. But, much as Luc wanted to remind her of what had happened between them, he was also relieved to see this version of her. It proved he had not been delusional in Nice—that this *had* been the woman he'd thought he was marrying. And he preferred that the world see only this: the capable, elegant princess, a credit to her country. And, of course, to her husband.

He would be the only one who knew the other side of her. His own, private, uninhibited princess behind closed doors. He nearly smiled at the thought.

"The rest suits you," he replied, rising and beckoning her closer, to take the seat opposite him at a small wrought-iron table. The housekeeper had prepared a tray—a selection of ripe, inviting Californian fruits and fresh-baked pastries. "Come. Do you take coffee in the morning?"

"Please," Gabrielle replied, settling herself into the chair with an unstudied grace that Luc found mesmerizing. She nodded her thanks when he poured her a cup of steaming black liquid from the carafe in the center of the table, and cradled the cup in her hands.

"It's a lovely morning," she remarked, and then talked for a few moments about the differences in temperature between Miravakia and Los Angeles, and her delight in the unexpected similarities between the two places—all in that same well-modulated, polite tone.

Luc recognized the fact that she was handling him with consummate skill—as if they were complete strangers seated next to each other at a formal dinner. Acting the perfect hostess, making perfect small talk to ease any possible awkwardness, smoothing her way into their shared morning with bright words and an easy tone.

She was a natural at it, he thought in satisfaction and some amusement.

He wondered if it was difficult for her—particularly today, when so much had happened between them the night before. He wondered how she felt—and then had to check a laugh at the notion that he, Luc Garnier, was concerned about a woman's feelings.

The last woman whose feelings had interested him at all had been his mother, and that had been an issue of survival rather than concern. Vittoria Giacinta Garnier had been as histrionic as her name suggested. She had tyrannized the household with her ever-shifting moods, making her feelings the centerpiece not only of her own life but of her husband's and her son's as well. Her gravitational pull had been like a black hole, sucking them all in.

"Does that amuse you?" Gabrielle asked, jolting him out the past. She placed her cup back on the table and folded her hands neatly in her lap. "I assure you I would not like to live so far from Miravakia, but I'm surprised to discover that Los Angeles is not as barbaric as I had been led to believe."

"And what of your husband?" Luc asked. He had promised himself that he would go easy on her, having misjudged her so severely. Yet the words seemed to come out anyway, despite what he'd decided. "Is *he* as barbaric as you expected?" He imagined she thought so, and yet somehow he could not bring himself to regret the events of the previous night, or her surprising innocence. Which was his now, to cultivate as he chose.

Color bloomed high on her cheekbones, making Luc toy with the notion that she could read his suddenly graphic thoughts. He rather thought her flush would be significantly more pronounced if she could.

"I had no such expectation," she said quietly. Then, with every appearance of serenity save her flushed skin, she adroitly changed the subject.

"You do that so well," Luc said. She raised her brows in question. Even that was faultlessly polite. "Divert the conversation from subjects you do not wish to discuss."

Genuine humor warmed her face then, making him realize he had not seen it before—which was, he thought, a terrible shame. She was beautiful. Stunning, with that smile—an authentic one, warm and real.

"A necessary skill for someone in my position, I think," she said. "It's often helpful to talk of anything and everything save the one thing the person you're talking to would most like to discuss." She swept her eyes down. "I believe that when men excel at it, they call it diplomacy."

"Do you enjoy your position?" he asked, not sure where the question came from and ignoring that last little dig. He was trying to merge the different versions of Gabrielle together into one: the perfect bride, nervous and skittish; the runaway paparazzi-baiting liar; the wild, excited woman who had trembled beneath him; and this gracious, elegant woman who laughed on the one hand and yet looked as if a tornado could not ruffle her composure. He was not sure how all of them could be the same woman. She fascinated him.

Like any other puzzle, he assured himself. He would figure her out, too, and then lose the knife's-edge intensity of his current interest in her. It was only a matter of time.

"I have been my father's hostess since I was quite young," Gabrielle said. She picked up her coffee cup again, and took a delicate sip. She tilted her head slightly, considering. "I have always been aware that we represent not just ourselves, but our country. I enjoy that." She looked at him for a moment, then returned her eyes to her coffee. "Do you do a great deal of entertaining? I imagine you must, as head of such a vast empire."

"No." Luc wished he had not spoken so quickly, so matter-of-factly, when he saw her stiffen almost imperceptibly in her chair. "But it is not only your life that has altered with this marriage, Gabrielle. Mine has as well. It is time I recognized some of the responsibilities that I have ignored until now."

"I would not have thought you were the sort of man who ignored responsibilities of any kind," she replied after a moment. He did not know what to do with the odd sensation that gripped him then, at her easy assumption that he was a responsible sort of man—and that she believed this with such casual certainty and so dismissed it.

"You must understand that when my parents died I was only twenty-three," Luc said, shrugging. "I had to seize control of my father's company or allow all that he had worked for to fall into the hands of others." He had no intention of telling her the truth of that battle—how many had betrayed him, how many lifelong so-called friends he had been forced to jettison. But Luc was not a man who looked back. He smiled. "I became quite focused."

"Yes," she said. "You are known for it. It is impressive. Even threatening, I imagine." She smiled, as if to lessen the sting of her words.

"I consider that a compliment," Luc said, lounging in his chair. "I have worked hard to be considered a threat."

"And you have achieved your goal," she said dryly.

She reached over to the table, putting her cup down and picking up a bright red strawberry—which drove any thought he might have had of responding to her dry tone out of his head. Luc watched her pop the dark red berry between her decadent lips, and felt himself harden in response. But he had decided that he could not use the powerful sexuality between them as a weapon against her—she was far too innocent for those sorts of sensual games. He had decided, as he fielded the usual barrage of phone calls from his office and enjoyed his morning coffee, that he needed to court his wife. Reel her in. Charm and please her. That had been his initial intention—until she'd run off from the reception. He was resolved that it was still the right thing to do, no matter how desperately, in that moment, he wanted to exchange that strawberry in her mouth for something he would find far more satisfying.

"No one believed I could manage the company…my father's holdings," he continued, trying to bury the urge to turn this breakfast into something far more sensual. "I was just out of university." His eyes connected with hers, and her obvious interest in what he was saying seemed to collide into his gut with the force of a blow. He shrugged again, expansively. "I do not like being told what I can and cannot do."

Only twenty-three back then, Gabrielle thought, *and already so formidable*. She frowned slightly when he stopped talking.

"I'm so sorry," she said. She searched his hard face and imagined she saw something there—something that hinted at the pain he must have felt. Though it was entirely possible she was projecting—*wanting* him to have a softness somewhere that she could relate to, to make it easier for her. There was no visible sign of softness anywhere on the body he maintained at the level of a warrior's physique. She swallowed, and continued. "Twenty-three is still very young. It must have been devastating to lose your parents like that."

"You lost your mother, too, did you not?" he asked, his eyes dark as he looked at her. He was so forbidding, and yet she was not as terrified of him as she had been before. What was this new, strange spell that made her relax slightly around him? She had not the slightest doubt that he was even more dangerous now than he had been before—it was her damned body again, making decisions without consulting her brain. Her body was relaxed—it simply wanted him near. Her brain was far more conflicted.

"Yes," she said finally, jerking her gaze away from his. Gabrielle remembered so few things about her mother—the caress of her hand against a cheek, the whisper of her fine gown against the floor as she walked, the faint memory of a sweet scent and a pretty smile. "But I was barely five. I have far fewer memories of her than I'd like. I imagine losing not one parent but both in your twenties must be much worse."

A muscle tightened in his jaw and he shifted in his chair. His dark gray eyes became, if possible, even darker. Gabrielle felt the shift in the air around them—the way the sun suddenly seemed cold against her shoulders, the way her stomach clenched in reaction to it. To him. But the difference today was that his ferocity was not directed at her.

"It was a difficult time," he said, his voice clipped. He frowned. "But the media frenzy which followed was far worse." His lips thinned. "Such cowardly dogs! So many veiled suspicions—so much rumor and innuendo. As if the truth were not tragic enough."

"That's terrible," Gabrielle murmured, careful to keep her voice quiet, soothing—because she had the feeling he would stop talking altogether if she interrupted him, and she was not entirely sure that if that happened he would not resume intimidating her as he had before. Why was she not more worried at the prospect? Or did she imagine that now that she knew exactly how dark and masterful he was, how he could devastate her—and how she would enjoy it—she would no longer be susceptible to him?

"In truth, there was a part of me that was relieved," he said after a moment, his gaze fixed somewhere in the distance. "I am not proud of it. My parents were focused entirely on themselves. They were not caretakers. My father was, I think, desperately in love with my mother. With her rages, her affairs, her demands. But she was never satisfied with an audience of only one."

Gabrielle had read about his vivacious, famously temperamental mother. Vittoria Garnier had been flamboyant, reckless and luminously beautiful—and, as such, irresistible to the tabloid press, who had fawned over her and skewered her in equal measure. No one ever thought about the child in these situations, did they? Not then and not now. No one ever thought to question what it might be like to see your parents' marriage ripped apart in such a public, horrible way. Your paternity questioned, your mother's lovers cataloged for all the world to see, your privacy up for grabs to the highest bidder with the basest intentions.

Gabrielle felt a deep pang of pity for the child Luc had been, growing up in the midst of such a circus.

But she did not dare to express that to him.

"You have a history with that one man?" she asked then. "The one outside the restaurant last night?"

"Silvio Domenico," Luc said, with disgust, his face turning to stone. "And before you ask, yes—he *is* the same man I was filmed punching in the face at my parents' funeral. 'Grieving Garnier Heir in Graveside Brawl' I believe the headlines screamed." His mouth twisted. "Such dignity. Such respect for the mourning process." She wasn't sure if he meant the tabloids or—worse—himself.

"What happened?" Gabrielle asked. She didn't know why he was talking to her like this, but she was fascinated by this glimpse inside of him. He was so intensely guarded, and yet he was sharing his past with her. Of his own volition.

"He is a piece of filth," Luc said, his eyes blazing. "He is not fit to be scraped from beneath a shoe!" He muttered something obscene in Italian. "But none of this can matter today. It is all in the past."

Not so much in the past, Gabrielle thought with a flash of insight, if the fact that her flight had landed him in the papers again had triggered so much rage. Was it possible that all that fury had not been directed at Gabrielle personally, but at the specter of his mother all those years before?

"I am so sorry," she said, then searched his face, wishing she had not heedlessly wandered into the minefield of his past that way. The fact that she hadn't known made no difference. "I had no idea when I ran that it would affect anyone but me."

Something passed between them, electric and intense. Gabrielle was aware of the wind chimes in the nearby trees, the faint sounds of traffic in the distance, but she was otherwise held spellbound by his commanding gray gaze, unable to look away from him.

"I accept that," he said at length, turning to reach for his phone as it rang, signaling the end of the moment.

He answered the call in French, excusing himself from the table with a quick word and moving inside.

Gabrielle watched him go. He moved with the same focused intent and leashed power that he did everything else. It was only when he disappeared from view that she realized she had not taken a full deep breath since she'd stepped out onto the deck.

She nearly laughed. It seemed her armor worked as well on Luc Garnier as on anyone else—which astonished her.

Because already you believe he is somehow superhuman, she chided herself. *He is only a man.*

But she remembered the way he'd touched her, the way she'd writhed in his arms, and she doubted it.

CHAPTER ELEVEN

GABRIELLE stood on the elegant terrace high over the city of San Francisco and watched as the last of the day sank over the horizon, the beautiful northern Californian city lighting up all around her as darkness claimed it fully. The sun took the warmth of the day with it, and Gabrielle shivered slightly as evening gathered around her. She pulled her silk wrap closer over her bare shoulders, but made no move to go inside.

She could hear Luc's voice echo from behind her, inside the library in the luxurious penthouse suite into which he had retreated to make some business calls. She was just as happy to take a few moments to herself to try to process the past few weeks. To try to breathe.

Had it been only a month? It seemed like so much longer. But it had been nearly four full weeks since Luc had appeared at Cassandra's front door in the Hollywood Hills and everything had changed. *She* felt changed. What worried her was that she couldn't decide if she had changed in the way she had feared so much—what if she'd lost her ability to discern whether or not she had lost herself? Didn't *losing herself* mean that she might not be able to tell?

Luc had arrived in such a fury, but the storm had passed during that long, exquisite first night. It was almost as if Luc had woken up the following morning a different man. He was not suddenly easygoing or relaxed, of course—he was still Luc Garnier, and Gabrielle imagined he could never be affable or pleasant as some men were—but he had changed. He had gone out of his way to be courteous—solicitous, even.

That same day he had swept Gabrielle off for an afternoon trip up the matchless California coast. He had taken her on a helicopter ride over pretty Catalina Island, then out to dinner in the charming town of Santa Barbara, with its mix of Spanish, Mediterranean and Moorish architecture that again reminded Gabrielle of her home in Miravakia. After a dinner of spicy Cajun food, a car had whisked them away, up into the foothills, to the luxurious San Ysidro Ranch, which managed somehow to be as unpretentious as it was elegant. Their exclusive and private cottage house had been a little gem, hidden away in the trees along one of the creek side paths on the ranch property.

And all the while, Luc had talked to Gabrielle as if she was a human being—his wife and not merely his newest business acquisition. Gabrielle had been in very real danger of being swept off her feet by this far more accessible version of Luc—until she'd discovered her own bags at the cottage.

"What is this?" she'd asked, momentarily confused by the sight of them. "Why are my bags here?" It would have been one thing to find a single overnight bag—but she'd seen her entire suite of travel bags lined up neatly against the wall.

"I had everything sent ahead," Luc had said, as if that should have been obvious. He'd studied her for a moment. "Will you not be more comfortable?"

"I do not need *all* my bags, surely?" Gabrielle had said, suspicion sparking in her gut—especially when he'd turned away from her and pulled out his ever-present PDA. "How long will we be away from Cassandra's house? One night? Two?"

"We are not going back," Luc had said, without glancing up

from the PDA in his hand. He'd scrolled through a message, frowned, then slid the device back into his pocket. He'd strolled across the room and fixed himself a drink, all without turning to see her astonishment. Suddenly the reality of her situation— of her marriage and her husband—had come flooding back to her. How could a single afternoon have so bewitched her? How could she have forgotten for a moment?

"Of course I have to go back!" she had cried. She'd refused to let the easy charm of the ranch cottage distract her. So what if there was a soaring wood-beamed ceiling and a stone fire-place with a cracking fire within? She refused to be seduced by *furnishings*. "You had no right to just…*decide* that I wasn't returning to Cassandra's house!"

"Are you angry that I did it, or angry that I didn't ask you first?" Luc had asked mildly, settling himself on one of the bright sofas.

He had seemed as perfectly at ease surrounded by the rustic Western décor as he had in Miravakia's grand cathedral. It was as if he molded whatever room he found himself in to his own specifications, and it had seemed to Gabrielle, glaring at him from beside the grand four-poster bed that dominated the room, as if the cottage had been created with Luc Garnier in mind. It was maddening.

"I am angry that you seem to have no regard whatsoever for my feelings on this or any other issue," Gabrielle had replied. Perhaps the shockingly romantic day had lulled her into a false sense of security. It was the only thing that could explain her sudden boldness.

"We are on our honeymoon, are we not?" Luc had asked, still in that mild way. But Gabrielle had felt a frisson of alarm— or awareness—skitter down her spine. There had been steel beneath his tone.

"I…I don't know…" she had said. Honestly. She'd sucked

in a breath and dared, "I've told you that I think this marriage was a mistake."

She'd expected the rage she'd seen the night before—the sardonic remarks, the intimidation, the blistering fury. But he had not done any of the things she'd expected.

"So you have," he'd said. He had been unreadable in that moment, only watching her from across the room. He'd risen to his feet, never taking his eyes from hers, and inclined his head. "The fault is mine, I think. Perhaps I need to concentrate on more exciting honeymoon activities than today's touristy adventures. Perhaps that would put you in a better frame of mind where our marriage is concerned?"

"I don't think *activities* are going to change the fact that I—" Gabrielle had begun, but her words had dried up on her tongue, because he'd pulled the tails of his shirt from his trousers with a quick jerk of his wrists. His dark brows had arched—challenging her.

"I beg your pardon?" he had said, his mild tone at odds with the sudden sexual heat that had filled the room. "You were saying?"

Then, still maintaining that disturbing, intoxicating eye contact, he'd slowly unbuttoned the shirt and shrugged out of it. She had been the one to blink, to let her gaze fall—indeed, she'd been powerless to resist.

Gabrielle had not been prepared for the sight of him in the cheery light of the cottage and the fire instead of the dark of the previous night's bedroom. His chest was all hard planes and fascinating dips, the wide expanse of his pectoral muscles narrowing to a tight abdomen and lean hips. Dark hair dusted his muscles, making him seem even more impossibly male. He was gorgeous. Beautiful. And Gabrielle had been seized with the urge to taste every bit of his golden skin that she could see.

But then he'd made everything even worse by raking his trousers off, stepping out of them stark naked.

"What are you doing?" Gabrielle had managed to whisper, while her heart had hammered at the walls of her chest and the blood had pumped so loudly in her ears she'd thought it might permanently deafen her.

He'd stood before her with arrogant nonchalance and without a shred of modesty. But then he had nothing to be modest about. Gabrielle hadn't been able to help herself—her eyes had been drawn almost against her will to that place between his legs that she had *felt* the night before—in the kind of detail that it made her feel dizzy to remember—but had previously only *seen* on sculptures in museums.

She'd gulped. If she'd been wearing pearls, she might have clutched them. His maleness had hung thick and proud before him, and as she'd looked at it, it had stirred to life. She'd felt her body respond—her breasts grow heavy, and that wet, coiling hunger roll to life in her groin, fanning out and lighting her afire. She had been fascinated. Her body had simply wanted him. Again. *Always.*

As if his male organ had read her mind it had thickened—hardening until it stood away from his flat belly.

Her eyes had flown to his, silver and amused in the firelight.

"I am going to sit in the hot tub out on the patio," Luc had said lazily. He'd reached over and picked up his drink, as urbane and sophisticated as if he had been dressed in full black tie. "Perhaps you would like to join me?"

Gabrielle had gaped at him, her breathing erratic. His naked body had been all she could think about—the sight of all that bare skin and maleness making her feel wild and mad and jittery.

"I've only been in a hot tub in the spa," she'd said. Idiotically.

"This will be different," he'd promised, amused. He'd held

out his free hand, commanding and regal, making her feel distinctly overdressed by comparison. She had wavered, her body clamoring for her to throw herself at him while her mind warned her that the bags were a lesson she could not afford to ignore—so peremptory and arrogant and—

But then he'd smiled. One of his rare, heartbreaking smiles. One that flashed that fascinating dent in his lean jaw and made his eyes gleam like highly polished platinum.

"Trust me," he'd said.

And she'd found herself moving toward him without another thought…

Gabrielle shivered on the terrace in San Francisco—but not from the cold. She darted a look over her shoulder, but Luc was still indoors. She could still hear his voice—the dark, rich caress of French when he talked to his assistants, the lyrical lilt of Italian when he spoke to his right-hand man.

She would never look at a hot tub the same way again.

And that had only been the first night.

Luc had hired a sexy little convertible and they'd meandered their way along the spectacular California coast, their bags turning up in one luxurious suite after the next in places Gabrielle had only ever read about. Big Sur, the Carmel Valley, Monterey. Gabrielle had hardly known where the rugged beauty of the California coastline left off and her husband's began. He'd made love to her every night, over and over, with a ferocity that had made her toes curl and her heart sing, the nights bleeding into the days until she felt as aware of his body as she was of her own.

He was more dark magic than man, she thought, and she knew she was spellbound, enchanted. Every night, she tried to resist him. Every time he touched her she tried to hold something of herself in reserve—to keep some small part of herself safe. But now as she stood with all of San Francisco laid out before her, she was forced to wonder what that small, hidden part of her mattered when every other fiber of her being seemed to dance to his tune at his command. How could she have allowed this to happen? Unlike her father, whom she had blindly followed for years out of a sense of duty and familial obligation, and her own helpless love for him no matter how remote he seemed, she had known immediately that she should not do the same with Luc. And here she was, a scant few weeks later, turned inside out because he wished it.

The worst part was, she could summon up only the most distant kind of alarm.

Did *she* wish it? Was she pretending to want to resist him while secretly thrilling to her own surrender? Was it not surrender at all, but instead the acceptance of pure, unadulterated pleasure—something she had never permitted herself before?

Something in her suspected that it might be true—though she shoved it aside.

Someday this spell will break, she told herself now, sternly, *and then what will you have? A marriage that resembles your relationship with your father much too closely. A life completely and utterly controlled by a man you never wanted, never chose.*

But she wasn't sure she cared as much about that possibility as perhaps she should.

"Gabrielle."

Just her name on his lips and her sex melted, while the rest of her body surged to attention. *Just her name.* He was lethal. She turned to see him standing in the French doors that led out to the terrace. He was dressed all in black—trousers, and a cashmere turtleneck that made him look impossibly French even as it clung to his spectacular chest, defining his lean, tight muscles. He frowned. It no longer made her heart beat in panic—but that didn't mean she had grown immune to him. Not by a long shot.

"There is a chill in the air, and a breeze this high up," he said. "You'll catch cold."

"It's a beautiful evening," she replied, smiling. She didn't move. It was one more little rebellion, hardly noticeable at all except to that tiny part of her she hid away, tucked deep inside.

The moment seemed charged, as the city rushed into night-time below them, bridges and buildings sparkling and spreading out in all directions. Gabrielle felt an emotion she could not name roll into life inside of her and begin to grow. She didn't know if that was what made her want to weep, or if it was the odd, arrested look in his eyes—as if he was seeing her for the first time. She swallowed against it.

"You look lovely," Luc said, crossing to her. He took her hand and lifted it to his lips. Even the barest touch of his mouth against the back of her hand made her quiver. And he knew it. She could see the sure, sensual knowledge in his silvery gaze.

It is only sex, she told herself, fighting her body's instant response. *Physical chemistry. It doesn't mean anything more than that.* There was no magic, no sorcery, no spell. He was just a man, and she had never explored her passions before. It was simple, really.

She'd been telling herself some version of the same story for weeks.

She wished she believed it.

"Thank you," she said, her voice hushed. She had dressed for the evening in a simple black sheath, and had secured her hair in a low, sleek ponytail, held with a jeweled clasp at the nape of her neck.

"I apologize for abandoning you," he said, searching her face as if he could see the struggle she thought she'd hidden from view. "I'm afraid my business does not lend itself to holidays, no matter how much I might wish it to do so."

Gabrielle smiled automatically—though she knew him well enough after these intense, close weeks to suspect that it was not the business that did not lend itself to time off, it was Luc himself who refused it. But she backed away from saying such a thing—from exploring the implied intimacy that knowing anything about him suggested. She had to keep something in reserve or she would end up with nothing. Why was that so hard to remember?

"I watched the sun set over the Golden Gate Bridge," she said, smiling up at him. Light, easy. Her polite hostess mode, all surface and shine. She clung to it—determined to feel as composed as she sounded. "How could I possibly feel abandoned?"

Her eyes were dark, with no hint of green—which, Luc had come to know over the past weeks, meant she was upset. She gave no other sign. Her smile was perfect, her body at ease. Yet he could feel her distance and he hated it.

"I am glad to hear that a sunset and a foreign city are adequate replacement for me," he said dryly, watching her closely. Her lashes swept down, covering her eyes, and when she looked up again he saw humor there.

"Was that a joke?" she asked.

"I never joke," he replied in the same tone, and she laughed.

"Have you concluded your business?" she asked, angling her body away from his as he moved closer. It was subtle thing—unconscious, perhaps—but Luc noticed it. He frowned. "It must be quite late in Europe."

"I decided to let everyone sleep tonight," Luc said. "But only because I expect them to work even harder in the morning."

She crossed her arms over her torso, pulling the wrap tighter around her body. She gazed out over the city, remote and beautiful. He did not see the city arrayed at his feet—he saw only her. He wished that he could penetrate her mind, explore her secrets. He had accepted that she had this power over him—a power no other woman had ever had. He had realized that he wanted to *know* her in a way that went far beyond the carnal. He assumed it was because she was his wife; knowing that he would be with her for the rest of their lives was reason enough to have a deeper interest in her, surely? He should have expected it. And like anything else, he told himself, this urge to know her would pass in time. It had to.

"Are you a good boss?" she asked, startling him. "Do they like you?"

Luc was incredulous. "*Like* me?" he asked. He rolled his shoulders back and frowned slightly. "I've never given it a moment's thought. They obey me, or they are replaced."

"I will take that as a no, they do not." Amusement made her voice rich.

"Is that how you plan to rule your country?" he asked derisively. "As a popularity contest? I doubt you will find that the most efficient form of government."

"There is a difference between fear and respect," she replied, seeming unperturbed by his harsher tone. It occurred to him that it had been a long time since he'd managed to get under her skin with only a few words. "Surely a good ruler should strive for the latter rather than the former?"

"This is all very naïve, Gabrielle," Luc said dismissively. "Yes, it would be delightful if my employees adored me. But what should I care if they do not? As long as they work hard, perform well and remain loyal, they are rewarded. If they wish to be loved in return, perhaps they should adopt a domestic animal."

She raised her brows, looking mildly quizzical. "You do not

care at all?" she asked. "You are perfectly content for them to hate you, so long as they perform their duties to your specifications? That is all you require?"

"I am their employer, Gabrielle." He did not understand why her tone set his teeth on edge, or why he felt suddenly defensive. Nor why she had developed this sudden interest in his business concerns. "Not their lover."

"I am not your lover either," she replied, a flash of anger in her voice, her eyes. "I am merely your wife. Should I hate you? Fear you? Will it matter to you as long as you are obeyed?"

He stilled. "You compare yourself to my employees?" he asked softly, watching her face closely. "Have you taken leave of your senses?"

"I fail to see the difference in our positions," she replied coolly. Whatever anger he'd sensed in the previous moment was gone, and she was once again composed and easy. She might have been discussing the weather forecast. She even smiled at him. "It is always best to know one's place."

The words struck at him, reminding him of the way her father had said much the same thing back in Paris. As if she were an animal, or a servant. He didn't know why hearing her repeat the same sentiment bothered him when he'd agreed with it before, more or less. It was unreasonable. Irrational.

Yet he still reached over and took her shoulders in his hands, pulling her to him, closing the distance between their bodies.

She came without objection, tilting her face up toward his, though he still sensed that distance in her, no matter how close she might be physically. She was too calm, too collected. Too damned serene.

He wanted her mindless, uncontrolled, *fierce*. The way she was beneath him, astride him. On the bed, the floor—wherever they happened to find themselves. He was becoming less and less tolerant of her smooth, perfect exterior when they were in private. She used it to keep him at arm's length, he was sure of it, and it infuriated him.

"I will indulge you anything you wish," he told her, holding her still. "Including this asinine argument you seem determined to have tonight."

"Are we arguing?" she asked lightly, her eyes unreadable in the night air. "My apologies. I was merely clarifying."

"But I must tell you," he continued, as if she hadn't spoken, "I had a very different evening in mind."

"Oh?" She was so unruffled. So calm. Why did that needle him? Wasn't a woman with her poise exactly what he'd wanted? What he'd searched for with such single-minded purpose?

Luc stepped back and reached into the pocket of his trousers. He pulled out the small jeweler's box, cracked it open, and held it out before her.

"A small token," he said quietly. An uncomfortable feeling gripped him. He scowled at her, still holding out the box with the damned ring—an impulse he suddenly regretted. But he still bit out the words. "I hope you approve."

CHAPTER TWELVE

His voice had gone stiff. Formal. He even scowled down at her, as if he wanted to shout at her.

In another man Gabrielle might have called it shy—even awkward. Odd that her poking at him about *her place* had had no such effect on him—but his giving her a gift did. Or perhaps it was the gift itself.

Gabrielle swallowed carefully and looked at the ring nestled in the box, with sparkle enough to rival the hectic flash and shine of the city all around them. She dared to raise her eyes to his, and what she saw there made a fine tremor snake through her.

He did not kneel. He did not mouth pretty words. He only gazed at her. It took her breath away. Not merely the ring. But the fact that he was giving it to her like this—like some kind of backward proposal for their backward marriage.

It was perfect, somehow. And she didn't know why it should matter to her. But it did. Oh, how it mattered—how it caught at her heart and squeezed.

"The stone belonged to my mother. The original setting would not have suited you, so I had it reset." Luc took the ring from the box and then took Gabrielle's hand.

She already wore the ring he'd put there in the cathedral on their wedding day, but this felt different—deeper, more emotional. Perhaps because she knew him now—knew his scent, his touch, the timbre of his voice. Perhaps because he might be many things she was still only beginning to process, but he was no longer a stranger.

Her hand felt fragile in his much larger one—breakable.

She found she was holding her breath as he slipped the ring onto her finger. It fit perfectly, as she had known it would. She spread her fingers wide to look at the new ring—feeling far too emotional to look at him in such a fraught moment.

The stone was a large diamond, cut to dance and shimmer with any hint of light. It sat high on a simple platinum setting, and looked as if it had been specifically made to grace and flatter her hand. Gabrielle had more jewelry than she knew what to do with—she had inherited her mother's pieces, and had the entire historical collection of Miravakian Crown Jewels at her disposal—yet nothing had ever touched her so much or so deeply as this particular stone from this particular man.

He doesn't need to do this, she kept thinking, bemused. They were already married. The ring seemed so…romantic.

A concept she could not get her head around. Not as it applied to Luc Garnier, the most sensual and least romantic of men.

"It is beautiful," she murmured, staring at it, her voice hushed.

It was as if the world had hushed, too, trapping them in a bubble with only this ring and unspoken undertones that made Gabrielle's body hum with tension or emotion—she wasn't sure which.

She didn't understand the rush inside of her that threatened to sweep her away. She was afraid to look at him—afraid she might succumb to the heat that threatened to spill from behind her eyes. But she forced herself to do it anyway, and felt the force of his gray gaze burn through her, kicking up brush fires all the way to the soles of her feet and back again.

His look was fierce. Demanding. And yet she knew, with a flash of feminine intuition, that despite appearances he was at his most vulnerable. Rather than making her feel as if she had an advantage, finally, it humbled her. Made her ache.

"It suits you," he said, in the same quiet voice.

"Thank you," she whispered, unable to say anything else despite the words that crowded in her throat, nearly choking her. She reached over and laid her trembling hand on his hard cheek, her palm caressing the place where that dent appeared on the rare occasions he laughed. She was not hiding anything from him as she gazed at him—she was wide open, undefended. More naked than ever before.

It shook her to the core. And yet she couldn't seem to look away.

"The car is waiting," Luc murmured after a moment. He turned his mouth into her hand and his lips curled against her palm. Gabrielle blew out a soft breath. He reached up and laced his strong, clever fingers with hers and gave her a crooked, almost boyish smile that broke her heart into pieces.

He does not have to do this…

But she gave no sign of her inner turmoil. She smiled, the way she always did, and followed him out to dinner.

Luc lounged against the leather seat in the back of the car and watched Gabrielle. Covertly. She extended her hand when he checked his PDA, tilted the diamond this way and that, so it caught the passing streetlights and sent light cascading around her. He was certain she did not want him to catch her in the act, since she dropped her hand into her lap the moment he slid the PDA back into his pocket.

"There has been a change of plans," he said.

"Our dinner plans?" she asked, turning that serene countenance toward him.

"No." He fought the urge to say something sarcastic, just to see if he could pry behind that mask as he had so easily in the beginning. More and more he was convinced he only saw the true Gabrielle when they were in bed. "Tonight we are going into Marin County, to a restaurant I think you will enjoy. An interesting take on classic French cuisine."

"It must be good," Gabrielle said, smiling. An expression he had not seen before—mischievous, he thought—crossed her face. "You are not just half-French, but half-Parisian, aren't you? Your palate must therefore be held to be even more discerning than a regular Frenchman's."

"Indeed," Luc said. Shadows hid her face, then bursts of light illuminated her as the car made its way through the city and toward the wild beauty of Marin County, just across the Golden Gate Bridge. "I believe I have been called particularly discerning even for a Parisian."

"I feel sorry for the chef," she said, clearly teasing him now, and Luc felt torn.

On the one hand he wanted her to continue looking at him with that bright humor in her eyes. He craved it. But on the other he was so unused to being teased that he wasn't certain what to do—how to respond in kind without becoming overbearing. And then, of course, there was the part of him that didn't mind being overbearing at all, if it would force her to open up to him and display her secrets.

He was not used to such indecisiveness.

"I had hoped to travel into the Napa Valley tomorrow," he said after a moment, casting the unusual feelings aside and concentrating on facts, as ever. "I have an interest in a vineyard there, and it is beautiful country. But I am afraid business calls me to London." He shrugged. "We will have to leave."

She was quiet for a moment. There was no sign of any frown between her brows, though for some reason Luc was certain there would have been if she'd showed her feelings more. He thought back to their wedding, and to that first night he had hunted her down in Los Angeles. Her feelings had overtaken her then, though she'd hidden them in public. When had she started hiding them in private, too? He didn't like the sensation that she was hiding *from him*, specifically. That there were whole worlds in her, perhaps, that he had no access to at all.

He should at least know that they were there. Shouldn't he?

"I have not been to London since last spring," she said at last. He felt certain that was not at all what she wanted to say. "Do you go there often?"

"Often enough," he said.

"I ask because, as I am sure you know, I have a residence there," she said. "If you would care to stay in it, we can. I don't know what your usual arrangements are in London."

He remembered, dimly, the house in Belgravia that had been mentioned as part of her holdings in the marriage documents. He was more interested in her periodic return to this stiff, chilly formality with him—though at least she had stopped talking of returning to her friend's house in Los Angeles. Did that mean she had accepted their marriage after this last passionate month? He found he was not willing to ask—and he didn't know what to make of such uncharacteristic reticence on his part.

"That will do," he said finally, when he realized she was awaiting his response. "I don't know how long we will stay." Was he afraid of what she might answer if he did ask? He dismissed that possibility. Since when had he ever been *afraid* of an answer, no matter how tough the question?

"However long you wish," she said. She smiled again. That

bright, easy, completely manufactured smile—the one she no doubt used on strangers. It was enraging. "I'll phone the house-keeper before we leave."

The civilized conversation was driving him insane. Luc wanted to reach beneath her manicured veneer and find the truth of her—force it out of her—so he could see it even when she sported all her sophistication and class like some kind of shield.

And then he thought, *why not?* Inside the car the barrier was raised, hiding them completely from their driver. The windows were tinted for privacy. *Why not, indeed?*

"Take off your panties," he ordered her, in the silken tone he knew would excite her.

She gasped. Color flooded her cheeks and her eyes widened.

"I'm sorry?" she said, her voice betraying her. It was husky as she tried—and failed—to summon up some outrage. "What did you say?"

"It is of no matter," he murmured. "I'll do it myself."

He turned to the side, maneuvering himself so that he knelt before her. He parted her long, gorgeously formed legs, taking care to run his hands along the elegant length of each, and kissing the curve of one knee.

"What…what are you doing?" she whispered, her voice ragged.

"You can leave your shoes on," he told her. He was tired of masks, of shields. He wanted the real Gabrielle. And he could think of only one way to access her—immediately. And if that also happened to go a long way toward rattling her compo-sure—well, that was even better.

His hands streaked up her thighs and hooked around the sides of the flimsy panties she wore. He met her gaze as he drew them down her legs, then over the delicate heel of each shoe—and watched her mouth open on a breath, though no words escaped. He held her eyes with his as he drew one leg over his shoulder, tilting her back against the seat, sliding her bottom toward him, angling her hot center toward his mouth.

"Luc!" A desperate whisper. "Luc, you cannot…!"

But he did. He kissed her calf, the turn of her knee, the creamy skin of her inner thigh. And then he moved into the cradle of her thighs and kissed the hot, sweet core of her, already wet and swollen and ready for him. He felt her go rigid beneath him. Her hands burrowed into his hair, her legs clenched around his shoulders.

He licked the length of her furrow, reveling in her scent, her taste. He sought out the center of her desire and sucked it gently into his mouth, then repeated it all. Again and again. Until she writhed beneath him, sobbing out incoherent sounds that might have been his name.

She was like cream and truth, all woman, and more delectable than the finest Parisian cuisine. He heard her moans and knew she couldn't fake that. He felt her body stiffen and shake, and knew with deep satisfaction that she couldn't smooth that away, hide it behind her manners and breeding.

She came apart around him, arching up from the seat and crying out his name, and he knew it was real. He could taste it.

He sat up, gently rearranging her on the seat next to him and tucking her against his shoulder. Her ragged breathing was the only sound in the car—like music to his ears.

She was his. Entirely his. He couldn't abide the idea that she was hiding something—herself—from him. He wouldn't allow it.

He reached forward and scooped up her panties from the floor of the car as her eyes opened and she blinked. She was bright red, and her eyes were heavy-lidded with leftover passion. He did not have to ask if she was satisfied—he could still taste the rich wine of her arousal against his tongue. She shot him a nervous sort of look, then reached out to take the panties from him.

"I think not," he said. He smiled as her eyes widened. He took the panties—a scrap of peach-colored silk and lace that she looked at in some mixture of horror and desire—and tucked them away in the pocket of his trousers. "We can both spend the entire dinner picturing you naked beneath your clothes," he said softly.

Her breath left her in a rush. A quick look told Luc that she was aroused as much as she was dazed, and that she didn't quite know what to do about either.

But as long as he could read her—as long as he'd shocked her public mask from her face—he didn't care.

CHAPTER THIRTEEN

WITHIN moments of meeting Luc's business associates—brothers from whom he had been attempting to buy a very successful chain of family-friendly hotels in various European Union countries for the past eighteen months—Gabrielle had them all eating out of her hand. Luc could not decide if it was the effortless grace of her manners, the quiet elegance of her subtly sophisticated ensemble, or some special Gabrielle mixture that only she could produce. Whatever it was, she used it well. She had the men and their wives at ease and laughing throughout the long meal in one of London's finest restaurants, seemingly without exerting herself.

She caught his eye as he watched her across the table laden with fine linens and delicate china, and he had the pleasure of seeing her gaze warm, though she made no other outward expression. But he knew it was for him only, that private heat, and it filled him with a sense of triumph.

No masks, no shields. Not when she looked at him. Not anymore.

"Your wife is truly a gem among women," one of the men told Luc in a besotted aside during the cheese course. He was the oldest of the three Federer brothers, and the most powerful. There would be no deal without Franz Federer's approval—

which was the only reason Luc had decided not to object to the way the man was staring at Gabrielle's figure, which she showed to advantage tonight in a sleeveless royal-blue shift. "Who would have expected the infamous Luc Garnier to take a wife, eh?"

It was clear to Luc that it was not the *fact* of the wife that stunned the man—but the *specific* wife that Luc had procured. It was equally clear that being called *the infamous Luc Garnier* was not exactly a compliment. Luc remembered Gabrielle's words about fear versus respect in his business, and wondered for the first time if she might have had a point after all. He had never cared much about the distinction. Maybe it was time he started.

"Even the mighty must fall," Luc said, with the wry shrug that seemed to be expected. He toyed with the delicate crystal stem of his wineglass.

"And lucky is the man who falls to a princess such as yours," Franz agreed, nodding. "Such graciousness! Such refinement!"

"I count myself lucky that I am old enough to appreciate both," Luc replied, ignoring the distaste that he felt.

He didn't understand it. He had wanted a wife who inspired this reaction in others—in men exactly like Franz Federer, in fact, whose well-known moral judgments about marriage applied only to others and never to himself. Luc had sought Gabrielle out for precisely this purpose. He'd found the single respectable woman alive who could inspire such raptures from usually dour businessmen. So why was he entertaining fantasies of planting his fist in the other man's face?

"Marriage is not for young men, it is true," Franz said, settling his considerable girth back in his chair. He patted his belly thoughtfully. His own wife, significantly and obviously younger than him, by at least two decades, had excused herself to powder her nose some time before.

Idly, Luc wondered if the woman was more interested in the waiter, who seemed closer to her in age and interests, than in her husband. She had been gone almost long enough to incite speculation.

"But it settles a man down. Even a man of your…ah… *stature*."

Luc had heard this before, of course. *Stature* being code for *reputation*. The truth was, he was feared because he was utterly ruthless. He knew no other way. When he wanted something— hotels, land, existing companies that he felt he could operate better, Gabrielle—he went after it. And he always got what he went after. Sooner or later.

"My *stature* precedes me, does it?" Luc asked mildly. He chose not to be insulted—he wanted the hotels more than he wanted to teach Franz Federer some manners.

He kept his gaze on Gabrielle as she charmed the younger brothers and their overawed wives with her stories of growing up in a royal palace not fitted for young children.

"I can't bring myself to tell you about the rock crystal vase I nearly destroyed one day, while playing horses in a drawing room," she told them, shuddering theatrically. "It's far too incriminating, and a priceless piece of art was *this close* to being lost forever! I would have died from the shame of it!"

She made it sound like a madcap adventure worthy of an Enid Blyton book, when, unless he missed his guess, a childhood with King Josef must have been anything but pleasant. He felt a kind of pang, trying to imagine her as a little girl, locked away in that *palazzo* with her grim, fault-finding father. He rather thought there had been fewer incidents of *playing horses* than the anecdote suggested. But her audience ate it up—captivated, no doubt, by the fantasy of a reckless young princess *this close* to disaster. Luc found himself no less charmed.

"I don't mind telling you that there was some concern that you might not be the best fit for our family's hotels," Franz continued, forcing Luc's attention away from Gabrielle and her past. "And with that business with the tabloids recently…" He shook his head sorrowfully, though his eyes were avid as he assessed Luc's reaction.

Luc smiled, though that deep, abiding rage he never seemed to conquer rolled over in his gut. He hated the tabloids. He hated Silvio Domenico and his slimy brethren more than he could express. He hated even more that Gabrielle had thrown them into the frenzy of a tabloid cycle—directly into Silvio's clutches.

But she had not planned it. She had simply run—afraid and unknowing. Luc believed her—and if he had paid closer attention to her emotional state at their wedding, and less to her father's assurances of her obedience, the entire affair could have been avoided. He blamed himself.

"You cannot believe what you read in those rags, of course," he said carelessly, as if it was of no matter to him. "They are writers of fiction and fantasy."

"All civilized men must be appalled at their prominence these days," Franz said, shaking his head in sympathy that Luc suspected was feigned. "The stalking and the lies. And yet everyone reads them!"

"They are a scourge," Luc agreed. He gestured toward Gabrielle. "As you can see, I have caught up to my runaway bride, against all the odds. Did I not read that she was tortured, somehow, by the experience? Ravaged in some way? I don't think she looks any the worse for her ordeal."

"Indeed she does not," Franz agreed. Perhaps too readily for Luc's comfort.

"The truth is that we honeymooned in America quite without incident." Luc sighed, sitting back in his chair and swirling the wine in his glass. "I wish I could tell you that it was scandalous, but it was not. I'm afraid my scandalous days now exist only in the imagination of the paparazzi. I cannot say that I regret it."

"I think she is a good influence on you," Franz said after a moment—as if Luc had *asked* to be patronized by a man he could buy and sell several times over.

Luc set his teeth and forced himself not to react. Every sense told him that this infernal deal was about to be closed.

"I would like to think so," he said. He even thought it might be true—though he did not intend to share that with Federer, of all people.

"You seem more settled. It suits you," Franz said.

The gall of it! As if he and Luc were intimate in some way beyond his lust for Luc's money—and possibly Luc's wife!

"This is good for a man as he approaches his middle years." Franz smiled. "And it will be good, too, for our hotels."

"I am pleased to hear it," Luc said. He extended his hand.

When the other man took it, Luc smiled. A real smile this time.

The deal was done. And Luc had his wife to thank for it.

She met his eyes once more, that telltale color reddening her cheeks. Suddenly, Luc couldn't wait to show her exactly how grateful he was.

London was a cold, gray slap after the sun-drenched blues and greens of the California coast. Gabrielle pulled her silk scarf tighter over her hair to ward off the wetness as she rushed through the Brompton Road crowd toward the doors of Harrods, eager to get inside and out of the rain.

Once through the grand doors, Gabrielle pulled her scarf away from her face and shook it out slightly, damp all over, though she found it a bit exhilarating after all the sunshine she'd gotten over the previous weeks. She had thrown a light trenchcoat over a pale yellow Chanel suit better suited to California than England, and was convinced she'd landed in a puddle the depth of the Thames in her rush to get from the car into the famous department store. She felt the wet and the London grime all the way up the backs of her legs. She was cold and soaked. And she didn't care in the slightest, because Harrods worked its usual magic on her the moment she stepped inside.

Gabrielle shook the water from her scarf and tucked it in the pocket of her coat, then unbuttoned the trench as she walked through the grand rooms she'd seen so many times before. She knew it was touristy at best, and sentimental at worst, but she had never been able to shake her abiding love for the British institution that was Harrods. Whenever she visited London she made a point to visit the store, to wander through the gilt-edged displays and marvel at the soaring ceilings and marble floors. Every now and again, when she knew her father would not be around to judge her, she brought home one of their gourmet hampers, always wishing she could take it on the perfect picnic somewhere, but making do with her private rooms. Being in the bustling, lavish rooms at Harrods reminded her of being a young girl, dispatched to the nearby store with her governess *du jour* while her father tended to affairs of state. Her father would have his privacy while Gabrielle enjoyed herself wandering about Harrods, then followed it up with an afternoon cream tea. Few things had ever made her happier.

"If it isn't the delightful Mrs. Garnier," a sly voice drawled in Italian from behind her, causing Gabrielle to start, and drop the leather gloves she'd absently picked up.

She recognized the man immediately—it was the paparazzo who had so angered Luc in Los Angeles. Silvio. He leaned close, his beard grizzled and the smell of old cigarettes wafting up from his damp jeans and tracksuit top. Gabrielle forced herself not to recoil—anything she did would be held up to scrutiny and twisted into the most negative light possible. It was best to do very little.

"My apologies, Your Royal Highness," the man continued, his voice suggestive, his eyes hard, "if I've interrupted. You looked so sad just then. So alone."

"Not at all," Gabrielle said easily, finding her public smile harder to come by than usual. "I was daydreaming quite happily, I assure you. I used to come here quite often as a girl." She swept him with a quizzical look. "Have we met?"

"Your husband did not introduce us when we ran into each other in Los Angeles," Silvio replied, shifting his weight to move even further into Gabrielle's space, water glistening in his shaggy salt-and-pepper curls. "But I'm sure you remember the occasion—outside a restaurant, just a few days after he chased you to the States? I think maybe he had something to hide that night, yes?"

"Something to hide?" Gabrielle echoed. The man obviously loathed Luc. It was etched into every line on his weathered face. She found she felt much the same about *him*. She forced a light trill of laughter. "I think you misunderstand him. My husband is a private man and we were on our honeymoon. No need to read anything into it but that."

"Private people don't spend their honeymoons having dinner at the Ivy, Your Royal Highness, do they?" Silvio retorted, so close now that Gabrielle could see the brown and yellow nicotine stains on his teeth.

She was forced to shift back against the display table to put an appropriate distance between them, and her skin crawled when he smirked.

"Not if they want it to stay private."

"You still haven't told me your name," Gabrielle replied,

buying time and scraping together every little bit of manners she'd ever been taught, determined to remain polite even when she wanted to run, screaming, into the streets of Knightsbridge to get away from the man. "I am afraid you have me at a disadvantage."

"I am Silvio Domenico," he said aggressively, and made a lazy sort of gesture with his hand, approximating a bow. He eyed her as he leaned against the display table, his cold gaze repellent. Gabrielle merely straightened her spine and waited. "I feel sorry for you," he said after a moment.

"I can't imagine why," she said crisply. Repulsive man! "But I must excuse myself. I have a great many—"

"I don't think you'll want to run off just yet," the odious man interrupted, with a smile that chilled Gabrielle to the bone. "Not if you want your so-called private husband's life to stay that way."

"What on earth are you talking about?" Gabrielle asked, letting her impatience show.

Sensing that he might be losing his audience, Silvio shifted closer, his gaze alight with an excitement that Gabrielle instinctively knew could not bode well for her. Or for Luc.

"It turns out that Luc's last mistress wasn't as discreet as she was supposed to be," Silvio told her with evident delight. He paused deliberately. "You do know that Luc is famous for his confidentiality agreements, right? No roll in the hay with Luc Garnier unless you promise not to talk about it. That's the rule. He makes them all sign." He waited for her reaction with obvious enjoyment—he wanted to feed on it, Gabrielle could tell. He wanted her to react badly—to hurt.

So she refused to show him anything, however little she might personally like to hear about the women who'd come before her. Much less any documents Luc might have had those women sign—which she very much doubted was true. Who would dare sell Luc out to the press? She merely arched an eyebrow.

"That seems quite sensible, given the fact you and your colleagues follow him around the planet digging for every detail," she replied crisply.

"What surprises me is that there are always so many takers," Silvio said, with that nasty edge to his voice. "Don't see the attraction myself." Gabrielle stared at him. He laughed. "You, too? I thought he bought you?"

"This conversation is over," Gabrielle replied icily, turning to go, but his hand on her arm stopped her. She stared at it, then up at him in outrage. How *dared* he touch her? "Remove your hand! At once!"

"You know about La Rosalinda, of course?" Silvio continued, but he dropped his hand. His voice lowered, becoming even more intimate and disgusting. "The toast of Italy. What an uproar Luc caused when he dismissed *her*!"

Rosalinda Jaccino was an Italian film star. She was a world-renowned beauty—all flowing black tresses, mysterious eyes and sexy curves. The sight of her breasts supposedly caused riots. She also happened to be Luc's most recent ex-lover. Gabrielle had read all about her while researching Luc in the weeks before their marriage. She certainly didn't want to hear what this repulsive toad of a man so clearly wanted to tell her about the other woman. Just as she really, truly did not want to picture that bombshell with her husband.

In bed with her husband. That sinuous, famously curvy body wrapped around his—

Those are not helpful images, she told herself dryly. And if Luc had wished to marry La Rosalinda he would have done so. Instead he had looked the world over and chosen Gabrielle.

But there was no time to ruminate on her marriage—she was trapped in the leather goods section of Harrods unless she wanted to cause a scene. Which she did not. She knew, somehow, that Silvio would stop at nothing to tell her whatever it was he had clearly tracked her down to tell her. She would just as soon he did not share whatever it was with half of London.

"What is it you want?" she asked with great patience, wishing she could escape into the Egyptian Hall next door. If this awful little man tainted her Harrods experience—one of the few truly happy memories of her childhood—she didn't know how she would stand it.

"It is not what *I* want," Silvio said. "It is what I think you will want—once you know what I know about La Rosalinda and your husband."

He made the word *husband* sound like a particularly filthy curse.

"Surely you did not come to talk to me about my husband's former lovers?" Gabrielle asked, with as much dignity as she could muster. "I must confess that I am not interested in them." She shrugged. "I am sorry if that disappoints you. And, while this has been a charming interlude, I really must—"

"Don't dismiss me, Your Royal Highness." The man's voice went cold. Brutish. His eyes were flat. "I don't think you'll be quite so high and mighty if I go straight to the papers with what I have, will you?"

"What *do* you have?" Gabrielle asked, fighting to keep her voice even. A trickle of foreboding ran through her, making her skin feel itchy.

"I have a tape." He laughed, still so close that Gabrielle could smell the tobacco on his breath, along with a hefty hint of onions. "Well, not exactly a tape. More digital than that— but the end result is the same, isn't it?"

"A tape of what?" Gabrielle asked through her teeth, unable to keep the edge out of her voice. The loathsome man was obviously enjoying himself. He tucked his hands into the pockets of his jeans and grinned at her.

"Your husband," he said, relishing the moment. "And La Rosalinda." He smirked. "The lady likes to film herself when she's in bed. And let me congratulate you, Your Royal Highness—your husband certainly knows what he's doing." He let out a wolf whistle, turning the heads of nearby shoppers. "He's the star of the show, believe me. Very accomplished."

"Don't be absurd," she said coldly, dismissively. "Luc would never allow himself to be filmed at all—much less at such a time."

"Who said she asked his permission?" Silvio retorted, his smirk deepening.

Gabrielle blinked at him. She held herself very, very still. Around them shoppers bustled this way and that, and London charged about its business, as if this wasn't happening.

This couldn't be happening.

"Why are you telling me this?" she managed to ask. But what she thought was, *poor Luc—this will kill him!*

"Unless you want the surround sound movie of your brand-new husband and his ex to air on television tomorrow night—so artistic—you better watch how you talk to me," Silvio retorted in a hiss. And then he laughed.

Vile little man.

"What do you want?" Gabrielle asked, hearing the strain in her voice as she spat the words out. Her hands curled into fists so tight she felt her nails dig into her own palms.

"Meet me back here tomorrow," Silvio said, with unholy glee in his voice. "Bring yourself, and ten thousand pounds—and I'll give you the tape." He laughed. "Bring anyone else—or tell Luc—and I'll sell the tape to the highest bidder and you can watch him perform with the rest of the world. Does that sound like a deal?"

Gabrielle could only glare at him—which made him laugh all the more.

"See you tomorrow, sweetheart," he said, and walked away.

CHAPTER FOURTEEN

"YOU seem unusually quiet," Luc said as the dinner plates were cleared from their places, sitting back in his chair and regarding Gabrielle with that piercing gray gaze of his. She was afraid he could see too much—see *through* her—too easily.

She tried to look at him and see what someone else might, but she felt too captured by his direct gaze to manage it. He was too virile, too masculine. The coat he wore was expertly tailored to emphasize the impressive, sculpted width of his shoulders. Across the dinner table his hard mouth crooked slightly at the corner, almost affectionately—a word she would never have thought to apply to him previously. The grand dining room of the London Ritz seemed to fade, and Gabrielle wondered helplessly if it would always be this way with him— if he would always command her attention, her focus, and bleed the light and color from the rest of the world.

She had an inkling that he probably would.

"I think that I miss the sun," she said, finding it hard to manage her usual light and easy tone. "Though this room is a fair approximation of it, isn't it?" She waved her hand, taking in the glittering chandeliers and lavish furnishings, all of which gave the famous hotel restaurant a distinct golden hue even late in the evening. "It's almost like sunshine."

She knew that she should tell him. She should have told him already. She should have called him the moment she'd left the horrible paparazzo's presence. She should have told him as they dressed for dinner—when he'd told her he preferred the slightly more risqué Balenciaga black dress to the more classic Chanel black dress and she had changed accordingly. She'd had ample opportunity to tell him during the ride from her house in Belgravia to the Ritz, when she'd asked him about his day and told him silly stories about her minor adventures. And they'd done nothing but talk throughout dinner—even touching briefly on his past with the paparazzi, giving her many an opportunity to raise the subject.

But every time she opened her mouth to tell Luc what Silvio had said—what he'd insinuated and what he'd claimed—she couldn't do it. It would hurt Luc too much. She didn't know how to tell him that his worst fear was on the brink of being realized. Wasn't this why he had chased her in such a fury to Los Angeles? He would do anything to avoid bad press—even that dinner he'd insisted upon in California, where they'd run into Silvio. And Gabrielle realized that while she was no longer afraid of her husband, she couldn't bear to hurt him—as telling him about Silvio's plans would inevitably do. He would rage and glower, and perhaps even threaten, but she knew enough now to know that it came from a place of pain. She simply couldn't stand to cause him any more pain.

The thought startled her. When had she reached that conclusion? When had she come to understand him that way?

"Sunshine in London, surrounded by rain and cold with no end in sight?" Luc said dryly, but there was a certain tenderness in the way he looked at her, and it tugged at her heart. "I suspect you are more of a romantic than you let on, Gabrielle."

"A romantic?" She smiled. "Impossible. There's not a romantic bone in my body. My father expressly forbade it."

"Shall we put it to the test?"

She didn't understand when he stood and stretched out his hand. She blinked at him in confusion. Then comprehension dawned, and she let out a startled laugh.

"You wish to dance?" she asked. "Here?"

Elegantly dressed couples already moved on the dance floor to the sounds of the four-piece band, but Gabrielle found it impossible to imagine the two of them among the crowd. It was so…so impractical. So very unlike Luc.

"Why not?" he asked, amusement making his silver gaze gleam beneath the chandeliers.

"Perhaps it is not I who am romantic?" Gabrielle murmured, and slipped her hand into his.

The last time—the only time—she had danced with her husband had been at their wedding, and Gabrielle found that she'd blocked out much of the experience in the chaos and excitement of what had followed. She tried to remember the details as he led her out on to a different dance floor, pulling her to him expertly. She remembered that part: the feeling of being caught up against the unyielding wall of his chest—of being held so securely she'd felt trapped, overcome.

She felt neither of those things now. Her breath seemed to tangle in her throat as she tilted her head back so she could look up at him—at the harsh, forbidding face that now seemed more dear and necessary to her than the mountains she'd stared at her whole childhood.

"The last time we danced was at our wedding," she said, aware that her voice was husky.

"I remember," he said. "You may recall that I was there and, unlike some, remained there as planned."

She ignored his dig. She even smiled.

"What I recall is that you lectured me about politically expedient spouses," she replied. She let her hand slide along his arm, testing the shape of his rock-hard bicep against her palm. "I think you meant to cow me into submission."

"Behold my success," Luc replied in a low voice, almost a growl. "I cowed you into a race across the planet."

"At your next wedding," Gabrielle said, concentrating on the part of her that felt the lightness between them, the teasing, and not the part that ached for him beneath it, "you might consider talking to your bride rather than lecturing her. I only offer suggestions," she continued hurriedly, when his eyes narrowed in warning, "because I know you are a perfectionist and wish to improve yourself in all things."

"Careful, Gabrielle," he warned, his dark eyes hard on hers.

She did not know if it was the teasing he objected to, or the idea of a second wife. He had proved remarkably and consistently ill-humored whenever the idea of an end to their own marriage—however fanciful—was raised. She decided to act as if it was the former.

"Come, now," she said softly, smiling. "We are none of us so grand that we cannot take a bit of gentle teasing, are we?"

"I prefer to tease in a more private place," he replied in a silky tone. "I find the results are far more edifying."

As he had no doubt intended, she could almost feel his mouth on her skin, his flesh against hers, the hot, hard length of him moving deep within her—and all while he held her so correctly, so reservedly, and executed the steps of the waltz with faultless precision. She let out a shaky laugh.

"Do not play games with me," he suggested, a smile lurking in his gaze though his mouth remained hard, "if you cannot compete."

She knew this was the way he played with her—and that she might be the only person on earth he could be said to play with. He did not know the meaning of the word *gentle*. He did not tease—he decimated. Everything about him—from the way he carried his hard warrior's body, fashioned for combat, in elegant couture, to the way he conducted his business affairs like the wars he did not fight, to this, his marriage—was the same. He was an unstoppable force—more machine in many ways than man. He knew nothing else, no other way of behaving.

She couldn't bear to hurt him. To cause him pain by telling him what Silvio had threatened to do. She was overwhelmed by the need to shield him, protect him.

And that was when she knew. When the truth of it hit her like a speeding train to the side of the head. She felt the blood drain from her face, from her extremities, so that everything tingled and hurt while her stomach clenched and twisted. An earthquake could have knocked her more firmly on her behind, though he continued to hold her up and move her about the room.

"What is it?" he asked, frowning down at her. "You look as if you've seen a ghost."

"No, no," she murmured, and tucked her head against his chest, because for once in her life she could not bring herself to smile. Everything seemed too sharp, too real—the world suddenly in brutal focus when she hadn't even known it was blurred. "I am perfectly well."

But that was not precisely true.

She was in love with her husband.

Recklessly, totally and heedlessly in love with him. Even thinking the word *love* made her blood pound harder in her veins and her head swim.

Of course, she thought, the truth ringing deep inside her like a bell. *Of course.*

How could she have thought it was anything else? How had she hidden the truth of it from herself for so long?

"Look at me," he commanded her.

She felt dazed, but she complied, letting that fierce gray gaze crash into her, knowing finally that what she felt was not terror, not panic, but a bone-deep exultation. It was hard and it was true and it was love—fierce and uncompromising.

She loved him.

"I am fine," she told him. Finally she smiled. "I promise."

"Do you need to sit down?" He was already moving toward their table, but she stopped him with a hand against his steely chest. She blinked to hide the sudden tears in the backs of her eyes. She was too emotional—too full with the sudden knowledge she'd been denying herself for so long. Too long.

"No," she said. "I want to dance." He looked as if he would ignore her. "Please? I am a little tired, I think. That's all."

He searched her face, and for a moment she thought he would remove them from the dance floor after all, but he relented. He pulled her close again, and frowned down at her.

"If you feel dizzy at all, tell me," he ordered her. "I am not a mind-reader, Gabrielle."

"Indeed you are not," she murmured, and he responded with something close to a snort. But he danced, sweeping her with him, gliding them both across the floor.

The band played; the chandeliers glowed.

She loved him.

Her body had known it from the first moment she'd seen him, as she walked toward him down the aisle at their wedding. It had overwhelmed her. Her blood had sung out to him, her breath had caught, and she had wanted him despite everything. Despite the fact she did not know him, despite the fact he had been so hard, so terrifying. Her body had known all along. Even while she ran, even while she hid, even while she tried to convince herself that there was something wrong with her.

She had called it weakness, worried she was going mad, tried to hold herself apart—but none of it had made any difference. He had managed to get to her, again and again, and she'd not only let him, she'd wanted him. She wanted him now.

But more than that, more than all the rest of it, she wanted to protect him.

She could not tell him about Silvio. She refused. She would do what she must and make sure Luc never heard about the tape. She would protect him from the thing he hated most, and she knew as she looked up at him, at his strong face set in those uncompromising lines, that she would love him desperately until the end of her days. Ten thousand pounds was getting off cheaply. She would pay twice as much, and as easily, to keep him from any more pain. She would do it happily.

"And now you smile," he said. "A real one this time."

"Take me home," she told him, her smile widening. "I think I'm interested in the kind of teasing you prefer."

As soon as the bedroom door closed behind them, shutting them away in the privacy of their suite of rooms in the grand Miravakian Belgravia house, Gabrielle turned and smiled—the kind of smile that made Luc harden instantaneously while desire roared through his body.

"My turn," she said. She seemed to shimmer in the glow of the single light left burning—the small bedside lamp she used to read, which cast the rest of the room into shadow.

"By all means," Luc agreed, tugging his tie off and opening the top button of his crisp white dress shirt. In his current state he would have agreed to anything. He couldn't take his eyes off her. She was incandescent tonight—radiant.

"You are so accommodating," she said, her eyes sparkling.

"You are different tonight," he told her as she swayed toward him, her figure displayed to breathtaking advantage in the formfitting black dress she wore so well. He'd spent the whole dinner fascinated by the delicate ridge of her collarbone. He was mesmerized now by the roll of her hips, the fullness of her mouth, the heat in her eyes. He was hypnotized.

She did not speak. She only smiled that same mysterious smile as she advanced on him and then put her hands on his body, making him smile in return with deep satisfaction because she was finally touching him. He made a low noise in the back of his throat as she ran her palms over his abdomen, then up his chest, leaving trails of sensation in her wake. She helped him shrug out of his jacket, then tossed it aside.

He nearly vibrated with a mixture of awe and lust as she sucked her full bottom lip into her mouth, worrying it, while her eyes moved over him, drinking him in. He felt it like a physical caress.

"Che cosa desideri?" he asked huskily. The room felt close and tight around them. "What do you desire?"

"You," she whispered, emotion crackling in her voice, across her lovely face. "Only you."

"You have me," he replied. Succumbing to a sudden sense of urgency, he backed her toward the huge raised bed that dominated the room as she yanked his buttons free, parting his shirt to stare greedily at his exposed skin. "You need only ask."

"I am not asking," she said, tilting her head up, heat and mischief in her gaze. "Tonight I am telling you."

"Is that so?" he asked lazily, enjoying her boldness.

"You do not like being told what to do, I know." Her lashes swept down, and then she looked up at him again. She was suddenly coquettish. She was delectable. "I want you to take off my dress."

Luc smiled. "I find that perhaps I do not mind it as much as I thought," he murmured. He reached over and smoothed his hands along her curves, feeling the heat of the skin on her bare shoulders. "There are certain things you can always order me to do."

Spinning her around, he unzipped the dress and peeled it from her, slowly exposing her creamy skin to his hungry gaze. He pushed the fabric down over the swell of her breasts as they surged against a bra made of lace and imagination more than anything substantial, then further, over the flare of her hips and the triangle of scarlet and lace that covered her mound.

"Your wish is my command," he whispered, lifting up the heavy coil of her hair and pressing his mouth to the place where her pulse throbbed against her neck. She smelled of flowers and spice and went straight to his head—with a spike of desire to his groin.

She surprised him by turning around in his arms, stretching up to press her mouth to his. She was like heat. A rich, addictive sweetness that was all her—only her—with an underlying kick he couldn't seem to get enough of. The taste of her wrenched the desire in his gut to an even higher pitch. He raked his hands through what was left of her elegant chignon and jerked her closer, flattening her against him. He felt the push of her breasts against him, the hard ridges of her nipples like twin points of delicious agony against his bare skin, and angled his mouth across hers for a deeper, better fit. He filled his hands with the sweet curves of her bottom, pulling her tight against him, her softness directly against his throbbing groin.

She felt too good. He could eat her alive. In one gulp. But she wanted her turn, and he wanted to give it to her.

She pulled away, her eyes dark in the low-lit room. Once again that smile curved her lips. It drove him crazy. He had the sensation that the worlds he'd sensed in her were there once more—just out of reach, hidden in plain view—if he could simply decode that damned smile.

He let her push him backward toward the bed, intrigued by the new determination that tilted up her chin and brought that gleam to her eyes. She kept pushing against him, and he kept letting her move him, until he sprawled back across the deep burgundy silk dupioni coverlet. He propped himself up on his elbows and watched her. If this was how she looked when he let her take charge, he resolved to allow it more often.

Very slowly, never taking her eyes from his, she reached behind her and released the catch of her bra—pulling it off with one hand and letting her breasts fall free. He did not move—he only feasted on them with his eyes. So close, and yet out of reach, the twin globes were begging for his touch—his tongue. Then she bent and slowly stripped her panties from her body, drawing his eyes along with her as she stepped out of them. One long, shapely leg, then the next.

Luc thought he might have lost the power of speech. He ached to bury himself in her. His hands twitched with the need to touch her. And she only stood there, for a moment that seemed to stretch into infinity—her eyes as unreadable as the sea they were said to resemble.

Just when his patience was about to snap she stepped toward the bed, running her hands up his legs until they met at the waistband of his trousers. Her hair trickled across his stomach—teasing him, inciting him, driving him slowly and softly out of his mind with the most intense lust he had ever experienced.

She leaned over him and set about removing his trousers with more single-mindedness than skill. She let out a soft sigh when she released his aching hardness from behind his zipper, and took it in her warm hands, testing the weight and feel of it against her palms.

Luc had to close his eyes and grit his teeth to retain control. Barely.

"Stop," he ordered her when she leaned forward, her mouth far too close to his sex.

He jackknifed up and pulled her away from danger, his heart pounding against his chest like a drum. He kicked his trousers off, wincing as he nearly unmanned himself in his haste to get rid of his socks, his underwear, without releasing his hold on her. Her hair fell around her in a tangled curtain of dark honey, her lips were swollen slightly from his kisses, and she was without question the most beautiful creature he had ever seen.

If he did not get inside her soon he might kill them both. And her mouth would not do—not tonight.

"I told you—" she began.

"I have only so much control," he gritted out, cutting her off, his own voice guttural in the quiet room. "I am only a man, Gabrielle!"

"Are you sure?" she asked, her laughter wicked. Powerful. Then her eyes darkened—a mix of passion and something else Luc could not identify. "I think you do not trust me."

She didn't give him a chance to answer. She climbed up on to the bed, straddling his thighs, bracing herself against his chest and holding herself there for a moment—poised above him, tormenting them both.

If he had meant to answer her, he forgot. He forgot everything.

"Gabrielle—" he managed to grit out, through his teeth.

And she sank down on top of him, burying his sex deep within her, making them both groan.

Luc pushed her hair back from her face and pulled her down close as her hips began to move in that delicious, mind-numbing roll that was uniquely hers. He kissed her once, twice, and then released her, watching her rear up in front of him like some kind of goddess. She rode him until they were both panting and she was moaning—rode him until she shone with the force of it—rode him with an abandon and an intensity that he had never seen before, never dreamed of before.

And then she whispered something he was too far gone in ecstasy to hear, and rode them both over the edge.

CHAPTER FIFTEEN

LUC had no intention of playing Silvio Domenico's demented games.

He'd received the paparazzo's call at half-ten that morning, told the vile dog exactly what he could do with his lies and rumors, and dismissed the matter.

Except here he was, a little more than an hour later, walking into Harrods like a puppet on a string.

He was furious with himself. He could not imagine Gabrielle doing the things Silvio claimed she was doing—the very idea was absurd. Gabrielle, who had little or no interest in the tabloids, selling compromising photos of the two of them to Silvio? It was laughable at best.

And yet he had come.

He had left a business meeting abruptly and hailed a black cab instead of his own car, all in his haste to confirm what he already knew to be a lie.

He knew Silvio. He knew how the man operated. He was outraged that the piece of filth had dared to utter his wife's name!

His wife.

She had surprised him last night. All that passion and abandon—and her boldness. He was stirred simply remembering it. There had been an intensity to their lovemaking that he hadn't understood, but he had responded to it—how could he not? She had bewitched him, clearly. There was no other explanation. He had chosen her because she conformed to a list of attributes he'd made up years before—but he had not expected this *thirst* for her. This ravenous hunger that he could not seem to satisfy.

Maybe that was why he had come? The hunger made him distinctly uncomfortable, as it did not fade or decrease. If anything, it had only gotten worse in the time he'd known her. He hardly recognized himself when he was around her. It was as if he forgot himself. He…wanted. He wanted things he found himself unwilling to name.

It would have disturbed him had he not been far too infatuated with her to care.

That infatuation was why he had come, Luc told himself. He was here to see through whatever charade Silvio intended to show him, make it clear the scum of a man was never to invoke Gabrielle's name again, and be on his way. Nothing more, nothing less.

He stopped in the designated place, lurking behind a display case like the paparazzi he abhorred. Why was he doing this? What could Silvio possibly have to show him that would make the slightest difference to him?

"I must tell you the truth about your wife, my friend," the other man had said, making Luc feel slimy by association, simply because he'd answered the unfamiliar number on his mobile phone. "Much as it pains me, you understand?" His laughter had turned into a hacking smoker's cough.

"How did you get this number?" Luc had demanded, disgusted.

"Does it matter?" Silvio had asked, with another arrogant laugh.

"I'm hanging up," Luc had snapped. "And then I'm having you arrested for harassment—"

"She's approached me with some naughty pictures of the two of you," Silvio had interrupted smoothly, with obvious lascivious enjoyment. "A souvenir from your honeymoon, yes? How proud you must be. I am told your—ah—*assets* are extraordinary."

"You expect me to believe that my wife wants to sell you photographs?" Luc had said derisively. He had made a succinct and anatomically impossible suggestion.

"Save it for your loving wife," Silvio had taunted him, unfazed. "And why shouldn't she make a little cash like everyone else? You're lucky she came to me. Anyone else and you would have seen it on the nightly news with the rest of the world. At least I'm giving you a little advance warning!"

Luc shook his head slightly now, and knew that his initial instinct had been correct. His coming here was a mistake. He had played right into Silvio's hands. The truth was that he *knew* Gabrielle could never conceive of such a thing—and she certainly would not be in cahoots with the likes of Silvio.

It was far more likely that Silvio was taking pictures of Luc now, as he lurked at this counter, and would later run some absurd story about it in one of the tabloids, claiming that Luc was meeting a lover—or something far more salacious. Drugs. Criminals. Who knew the depths to which Silvio might sink? He was less than a pig.

Luc was disgusted with himself.

But then he saw her, and he froze.

Gabrielle strode into the hall, looked around, and then marched directly toward the far side. She was so elegant, so refined, dressed all in snowy white. She held herself like the queen she would be one day. *What was she doing here?*

But he knew. He couldn't believe it, but he knew.

Another figure detached itself from the shadows and met her. Silvio.

It took only moments. Gabrielle held out an envelope and snatched the one that Silvio offered directly from his hand. They exchanged only a few words. Then she turned and walked away from him, exiting the store without ever looking around. She had no idea that Luc was there.

Silvio looked in Luc's direction and shrugged, his cocky grin firmly in place, but Luc barely noticed him.

Something broke loose inside him—something sharp and jagged and dangerous. It moved through him like a howl, though he did not make a sound. It was happening again. Just as it had happened when he was a boy. The frenzy of lies, speculation—the dirt that would slime him by association and follow him like a storm cloud.

And *she* was the one doing it this time. Not his parents—forever mysterious to him, forever unknowable and lost to him. Not them, but Gabrielle. The one he had chosen because she would never do this. The one he had believed would never, *ever* do this.

He should have known better than to trust her public face—the one that had tricked him into marrying her, the one that had deceived him even after he'd had to chase her across the globe, humiliated by her defection in front of all the world. She was no better than his self-centered mother—and hadn't he known that from the first? Hadn't he expected this behavior from all the women he'd dated across the years? The more beautiful they were, the more treacherous. Hadn't he known that since he was an infant?

He hadn't realized how much he'd expected—needed—her to have nothing to do with Silvio's little demonstration until he'd seen her walk in. He hadn't realized how much he'd trusted her until he'd watched her betray him.

He hadn't known how much he could feel, no matter how little he wanted to feel.

And it had never occurred to him that his heart might be involved at all until now, when it reminded him of its existence by aching like an open wound that would never heal.

The moment Gabrielle walked into their rooms and saw Luc already there she knew something was wrong. She stopped in her tracks and stared at him.

Luc sat in the sitting area near the large fireplace, his long legs stretched out in front of him and his arm thrown out along the back of the sofa that he seemed to dwarf. He wore a dark charcoal sweater that hugged the fine muscles of his torso and a pair of dark trousers that fit him exquisitely, emphasizing his strength and power. He looked gorgeous, as ever, and his position suggested relaxation and ease, but Gabrielle stiffened. She could feel the dark tension emanate from him in waves. His gaze—cold, and a dark gray too close to black—locked to hers like a slap. A shiver of anxiety slithered along her spine.

She had not seen that particular look of his in a long time. Not since the night he'd appeared at her door in California, in fact. And she did not remember him being quite so hostile even then. She was surprised to discover he could still make her gasp in reaction simply with the force of his gaze.

"Has something happened?" she asked at once. She crossed to him, sinking down into the plush armchair facing him.

Foreboding and menace seemed to fill the room, and all he did was look at her, as if he was trying to read her. His rugged face had closed down, turned back into stone and iron—and he was once again the forbidding, menacing stranger who had so overwhelmed her originally.

She realized with some amazement that she hadn't understood how much he'd changed—how open he had become, how relatively warm and approachable—until now.

"Did you have a nice day?" he asked, in that low voice with its treacherous undercurrents. She couldn't read him at all—but she could sense that she should tread carefully, even so.

"Yes, thank you," she said automatically, her ingrained politeness kicking into gear despite her confusion. "I saw some old friends for lunch. It was lovely. And you?"

How absurdly formal! Gabrielle felt ridiculous—and then his mouth pulled to the side in obvious mockery, and the feeling intensified. She felt color high on her cheeks as his gaze—insulting and cutting—swept over her, leaving marks, she was sure.

"I, too, saw an old friend of sorts," he murmured. His tone sharpened as he leaned forward, no longer pretending to be casual. His gaze slammed into her. "Tell me, Gabrielle—and please do me the favor of being honest, if you can—where are they?"

"Who?" she asked, confused and wary.

He thought she was dishonest? She felt skittish and nervous in a way she had thought never to feel around him again. It turned out that loving him did not change the way he could get under her skin. Perhaps love only explained it. It was an uncomfortable notion.

"My friends?" she continued when he did not. "They are distant cousins, actually, and we met in Chelsea—"

"Not your friends."

His voice could have cut through steel. She nearly winced, though she caught herself. She ordered herself to calm down, to keep talking.

"Why won't you tell me what's happened?" she asked. "You look… You look so—" She broke off helplessly. What could she say? *You look as hard and remote and cold as you used to be—before I knew I was in love with you, before I believed this marriage would work?* She didn't know what was going on, but she knew that this could not possibly be the right moment for that revelation.

"You should be less concerned with how I look," he bit out, his big body seeming to vibrate with all the leashed power she could sense he wanted to release, "and more concerned with what I am about to do."

Gabrielle blinked. That was obviously a threat. But why? What could he imagine she'd done? She thought of the repugnant Silvio and their exchange at Harrods—but even if Luc knew of it, why would he take his anger out on her? Surely she was an innocent party in that mess?

"I don't know what you mean," she said, folding her hands in her lap and straightening her spine as much as she could, thinking that if he would not simply tell her what was going on she would wait him out. Hadn't she already decided that was the smartest way to handle him? He would destroy her in any straightforward contest. She wasn't sure he could help himself—that was his way. Her best bet was to endure, and wait. She had every faith he would come around in time. And that she was more than capable of surviving the storm until he did.

"Do you think your manners will help you?" he asked in a near sneer, his eyes boring into her even as he held himself firmly in check. "Do you think I will be fooled?"

"Luc, please." She searched his face, but the Luc she had come to know was gone, and in his place was this creature of granite, of glaciers and stone. As much a stranger to her as he had been on their wedding day. Her heart began to beat out a jagged, panicked rhythm. *No one said it would be pleasant to wait out the storm,* she thought. "I can't defend myself if I don't know what you're talking about!"

"Where are they?" he thundered, making her jump.

"I don't know—"

"The pictures," he bit out, fury etched across his face, making him seem as deadly as the warrior she'd sometimes fancied him to be.

"Pictures?" Had he gone mad? She had not the slightest idea what he could be talking about. She blinked at him. "What pictures?"

He launched himself up and onto his feet. Gabrielle's heart leapt to her throat—but he did not reach for her. She did not know if she was glad of that or not. He paced around the room, looking like some kind of elegant wild animal, all rangy motion and lethal energy. She stood, too, thinking it best not to have him behind her or out of sight, as any animal of prey would in the presence of so unpredictable a predator.

"The camera must be automated—and portable, obviously," he said, addressing the room in general more than her, still in that low, tense voice. "You had nothing to do with our hotel arrangements, so you could only have had moments to prepare it and put it into place. But I can't find the damned thing and I can't find any pictures." He turned back to her, his gaze flicking over her contemptuously. "But you already have what you want, don't you? Your final rebellion against your father— against me—accomplished with a few clicks of a camera lens."

"Luc." She said his name softly, trying to sound reasonable. "You are not making any sense."

His head tilted to one side, an arrogant and challenging gesture, and his eyes ran hot with molten fury—and it was directed at her. Gabrielle felt her breath hitch in her chest.

"Am I not?" he asked. Too quietly. Too precisely. Biting the words off with his teeth. "Let me tell you what does not make sense to me. The money. Why would you need it? You have your own. And even if you did not—"

"Money?" Gabrielle shook her head, warding his words away from her. "You think I am motivated by *money*? Like some desperate—?"

"Even if you did not," Luc gritted out, ignoring her, "I have more than enough money to keep you in any style you wish. So it cannot be for money. What else could motivate you? Are you not famous enough? Photographed enough? Do you aspire to the ranks of those interchangeable starlets known only because they have no shame, no lower place to fall? Or is it one last rebellious act from the supposedly obedient princess? *Tell me!*" he demanded, louder, moving closer, yet still maintaining his distance—just outside an arm's length away.

As if he was afraid to touch her, she realized in astonishment. Was he afraid that he would hurt her? Or did he want to? Or, like her, did he suspect that if they touched his anger would disappear in the heat of their need for each other?

"I have no wish to be any of those things," she said softly.

"At first I simply wanted to destroy you," he told her, in a voice that was almost affectionate—though his eyes glittered dangerously and she knew better. "To cast you out and be done with this farce. But I cannot figure it out, Gabrielle. I cannot make sense of it."

"What do you think I've done?" she asked, holding herself still, or unable to move, perhaps, while he looked at her that way. Her breath hurt her, sawing in and out of her lungs.

"I know what you've done," he said bitterly. He shook his head. "But you were a virgin—you could not have faked it. I am sure of it." He let out a hollow sort of laugh. "Why I equate virginity with honor, I do not know. At the end of the day you are still a woman, are you not? Perhaps you planned this from the start."

Gabrielle blanched at the bleakness in his voice, then shook her head. She racked her brain for any possible issue that could have upset him this much, but couldn't think of anything.

Except her meeting with Silvio.

"There *is* something I haven't told you," she said, fighting to remain calm—or at least sound calm. "But even if you know about it, I don't know why you should be so angry with me. I thought I was doing the right thing."

"Did you?" He sounded only mildly interested—halfway to being bored—but Gabrielle knew better. She knew this was Luc at his most lethal.

"Yes," she said. She felt her confusion melt away in a rush of overdue anger that punched into her gut and hummed through her—how *could* he speak to her this way? After they had come so far? Had he been pretending all this time?

"You call this the right thing?" he said, with a nasty, sardonic inflection that made her want to slap him—an urge she had never had before in her life. "You can say this to my face?"

"Of course," she said tightly, and lifted her chin.

He could go to hell—with his anger and his coldness and this insane line of questioning, as if she was a common criminal. Who did he think he was? And here she was, so in love with him—it was infuriating.

Her hands balled into fists. She raised her eyebrows in challenge. "Of course I thought so. Why else would I meet with Silvio?"

CHAPTER SIXTEEN

"So you admit it." Luc could not believe it. He could not believe she would *defend* what she had done! He felt frozen, and yet nearly liquid with fury—all at the same time. He felt as if everything shook—as if the city of London wavered beneath his feet—but nothing moved. Not even him. "You do not even try to lie to protect yourself? You announce it freely!"

Her gaze darkened, her mouth flattening into a thin line.

"I don't know what you want me to say." She crossed her arms over her chest. Hugging herself tight or fending him off? He couldn't tell. "Why engage in this exercise? Why not simply ask me about it if you already know?"

"This is how you respond?" He was so angry he felt his hands twitch and his blood pound against his temples. His suspicion that she had planned this from the beginning—first his humiliation when she disappeared, then this betrayal to the vile tabloids just as he began to trust her—crystallized in the vicinity of his chest. "This is your defense of something so low, so disgusting, that it demeans us both?"

"I thought I was helping you!" She enunciated each word, showing her temper, no longer so perfectly composed. But even that added to his fury. *Now* she showed him cracks in her well-mannered façade? Now, when it couldn't—shouldn't—matter any longer?

The emotions he'd spent his entire adult life avoiding filled him now, in a churning mess, and they were as unpleasant and unhelpful as he recalled. Anger. Hurt. What was the point of either? He tried to wrestle the emotional wave that crested inside of him into line—to tamp it back down beneath the smooth exterior he'd worked so hard to have define him—but it was too late. He had the sudden notion that he and Gabrielle were the same—with the masks they each wore, the calm surfaces with so much hidden beneath. Too much hidden.

And what does it matter now? he asked himself bitterly. She was the one he had trusted. She was the one he had married. And yet it turned out she was the same as all the others, the same as his deceitful mother—worse, because he had believed better of her. Because she had somehow convinced him that she *understood* him. What had he been thinking?

"You thought you were helping?" He had to turn away before he did something he would truly regret. Like show her these things he didn't want to feel—all of them, in all their raw and vulnerable ugliness.

No. He would not. He could not bear to be so exposed. Not now, not ever—and certainly not after she had so betrayed him. *No.*

"Yes, I thought I was helping." She blew out a ragged breath. "Why else?"

When he turned to look at her again she had pressed her fingers to the frown between her eyes. She rubbed at it, then dropped her hand to her side. She regarded him warily, her eyes too wide and too dark—as if *he* had wounded *her* somehow!

"Silvio approached me yesterday," she said quietly. "He told me your—that there was a tape."

"Stop," Luc ordered her with a slash of his hand through the air, as if to cut her words off himself. The chaotic emotions inside him intensified—burned—fought to come out. "I cannot hear any more lies!"

"Lies?" She raised her gaze to his, anger and confusion and something else mixed together in the blue-green depths.

"I don't know what I was thinking," he raged at her, his voice like a low, angry throb in the otherwise hushed room. He could feel his own vulnerability like a sharp pain, and he hated the fact that he could not control it—could not control himself. Hated more that she had brought him to this. That she had *planned* to do this to him, and now stood before him and denied it. "I have become everything I despise. That is what is most clear to me in all of this. I am no better than my father in his day, dancing to her tune—"

"I am not your mother," she interrupted him. Her voice was even, her eyes steady on his. But he ignored her.

"This—this—*infatuation* has made me a stranger to myself," he continued, as if she hadn't spoken.

He had been bewitched, enchanted—but these were simply other ways of saying he had been played for a fool. She had played him—he who had never let his guard down before. And look what happened when he did! When he made romantic gestures to a woman who had run away from him at his own wedding! Anger. Hurt. Fear that now he had let these emotions out they would rule him. That he would become a slave to them, like his parents before him.

He had the terrible notion that it was the fact that *she* had done this that hurt—not simply that it had been done. That *she*, Gabrielle, was no different from the others. He had trusted her more—he had liked her more—

"But no more," he snapped. *No more*, damn her.

She moved toward him then, her frown melting from anger to cautious concern. She reached out to touch him—but he intercepted her hand before she could make contact with his cheek and held it out between them like a weapon. Hers or his, he did not know.

"*Je sais exactement ce que vous êtes—plus jamais ne me tromperez-vous,*" he spat out. "I know what you are, Gabrielle. I won't be fooled by you again."

"Luc—"

"This is over," he threw at her.

Even to his own ears the words sounded as if they came from far off—some faraway rage, someone else's fury. Better that than the keening mess in his gut, his fury like some kind of flu, ravaging through his body. How could this be happening to him?

"This marriage should never have happened. I should have known that no one could live up to my standards. That even in Nice you were nothing more than a carefully constructed lie. Did your father plan it? Or was that you, too?"

He could feel her pulse flutter wildly in her wrist.

"What…? Nice?" she asked, reeling. "What would my father have to do with—?" She cut herself off, trying to make sense of his angry words. "You were in Nice when I was? This past spring?"

"I followed you," he told her, without a shred of apology, forcefully—wanting to rip into her with the knowledge. Anything to make her hurt as he hurt. Anything to ease the force of it inside his own body. "I wanted to make sure you had no skeletons in your closet—no secret lovers, no dirty laundry. What does it matter now? You never saw me then, and believe me, Gabrielle, you will never see me again."

He saw the color drain from her face. He wanted to soothe her pain even as he caused it. He wanted to pull her close and crush her mouth to his. He wanted her even now, and he hated them both for it.

"You cannot mean that!" she cried.

He watched her pull herself together—he wondered what it cost her.

"This is crazy—a misunderstanding—"

"I want an annulment."

The words fell between them like stones from a great height. Gabrielle flinched, her eyes wide and shocked.

"But you... We..." She couldn't seem to form sentences. She cast around for words, her mouth working, her eyes glued to his. "We cannot *annul*, surely—?"

"I have already contacted my lawyers," he told her, taking satisfaction from the way his words hit her body like blows, making her falter on her feet. Though he still held her hand in his—a pale imitation of the way their hands had once touched and would never touch again. Why did thinking that deepen his pain? Where was the indifference that should accompany his realization that she was as fake as the rest—as untrustworthy, as disappointing? "I suggest you do the same." He sneered at her—anything to create distance, to make her like the others. "I will be claiming fraud, of course."

"Luc—" She had to clear her throat, and she sounded like a stranger, hoarse and choked. "Luc, you cannot do this."

"Why can't I?" He moved close—too close, tempting himself with the wild madness of her mouth so near to his—and bared his teeth. "You abandoned me on our wedding day. You besmirched my name across the globe. You are no better than the paparazzi scum you are so friendly with. I have no doubt you planned this with them for the maximum amount of embarrassment." He remembered he was holding on to her hand and let go of it abruptly, releasing her so she stumbled backward. "You are nothing to me."

"But—but—I love you!"

She gasped even as she said it—and her hands flew up to cover her mouth, as if she could stuff the words she'd cried back inside. Her breath came in agitated pants. Her eyes were dark and glazed with emotion, but he wanted more. He wanted her to deny that she could ever have dealt with Silvio—could have sold him out. Barring that, he wanted her to hurt, to howl. He wanted to make sure she felt every bit as empty as he did.

"I beg your pardon, Gabrielle?" He snarled her name like the snap of a whip against tender flesh. "What did you just say?"

But she surprised him. She curled her hands into fists again, and then dropped them to her sides. She was still dressed in pristine, snowy white, the only color her overbright eyes, like the sea in a storm. The cowl neck of the top she wore showcased her delicate collarbone and the elegant line of her neck. He hated that she could look so beautiful, so regal, even now.

"I said that I love you," she said, her voice thick but her head high. Her eyes glittered, but stayed steady on his. "I do."

"You *love* me?"

It was as if she'd spoken in one of the few languages he didn't know. He pronounced the word *love* as if it were some kind of disease, as if he could be infected by saying it aloud. Inside him, something broke. He felt it—felt the rising tide of an emotion like grief that accompanied it. But he could not allow what he feared would follow any acknowledgment that her words had gotten to him. *He would not.*

He cocked his head to one side and looked at her as a snake might look at a mouse. "And what reaction do you expect me to have to this convenient announcement, Gabrielle?"

"I have no expectations." He saw her throat work. "It is no more and no less than the truth."

He let out a filthy Italian curse that made the color flood her face. Then he closed the distance between them, his palms wrapping around her bare shoulders and hauling her to him, bringing her face scant inches apart from his.

Was it love or was it madness? Or was love itself madness, as he had always believed, though he had never felt as mad as he did now? Why did he yearn to touch her, again and again, stripping them both naked and sorting it out with their bodies? It was only sex, he told himself desperately. It had to be.

"You love what I can do to your body," he snapped at her. "You love the way I make you feel. That is all. That is *nothing*!"

"I can't help what you think," she whispered back, a sob in her throat. "But I do love you. Even now."

"I am touched, Gabrielle, but somehow unimpressed with such a brave declaration at such a time," he bit out, his fingers digging into her soft flesh, though she made no sound of protest. He bent her backward in some grotesque parody of a kiss—and he loathed himself because he wanted to kiss her, to lose himself in the heady insanity of her taste, her body. "You can explain to your father that you love me—and that is why you betrayed me, that is why I am throwing you back to him like something defective."

"Luc…"

Finally. Finally her tears spilled over and flowed down her cheeks. He exulted in them—and wanted to reach inside himself and physically rip out the part of him that still wanted to protect her, despite everything.

Despite what she had done to him. Despite how little she must care for him and about him if she could do it—if, as he believed more and more with each second, she had planned this from the moment her father told her she was to marry. And there was no mistaking it. He had seen her sell him out with his own eyes.

"I would never betray you! I love you!" she cried.

How could he want so urgently to believe her—even when he knew better?

"You and your love can go to hell," he told her, with cold,

brutal finality. He didn't know where it came from—but the coldness was like a savior, descending upon him and muting the turbulent mess inside him. Masking it. He forced himself to let her go. He stepped away from her and told himself he didn't care when she sank to the plush carpet before him, the marks from his fingers standing out against the pale white silk of her skin.

He had to leave her before he lost himself. That much was perfectly, terrifyingly clear.

He walked out, and he forced himself not to look back.

Gabrielle did not get up from the carpet for a long time.

It seemed to take forever for her to accept that Luc had left her—left the house, left London, *left her*—and even so, she did not fully come to terms with it until a full two weeks had passed.

He did not answer his mobile, and he did not return. He'd sent staff to collect his belongings within twenty-four hours of his departure—none of whom acknowledged her beyond a stiff announcement of their purpose. But she was still holding out a kind of desperate hope—something her father crushed in one short telephone call to London.

"You might as well come home," he barked into the phone, his displeasure evident even from as far away as Miravakia. "Your antics have lost you your husband, it seems. Best ensure they do not also lose you your throne."

Gabrielle couldn't think of any reason to stay in London if Luc had already started the process of dissolving their marriage. What would be the point? She might as well be in Miravakia as anywhere else—what did any of it matter?

She did not realize that she was in some kind of shock until she found herself back in Miravakia, ensconced in her father's *palazzo* as if she had never left. She had the sense that she was suspended in some kind of bubble, underwater, far away from whatever happened around her. In the middle of the night, when she could not sleep and could only lie awake, her body in a fever and her heart pounding with the enormity of her loss, she knew that she was hiding from the pain of Luc's desertion—afraid to really let herself feel what she was not at all certain she could survive.

She might have remained there forever—hidden away, protected, distanced entirely from what she shied away from feeling—had it not been for her father.

"You have proved yourself useless and ruined your reputation, so there can be no more trading on it," King Josef said one morning at the breakfast table, when Gabrielle had been home for some weeks. If he had broken his customary silence before, Gabrielle had not noticed. "I'm afraid I don't possess the necessary imaginative prowess to make a silk purse out of this sow's ear."

She realized two things simultaneously as she stared down at her bowl of muesli, his cold, brutal words falling around her like so many blows. One, that this was not the first time her father had spoken to her like this—not by a long shot, and this was not even the worst example of his cruelty or his callous disregard for her feelings. And two, she was not required to listen to it.

A part of the hard shell she'd gathered around herself cracked wide open.

She was done with it. With him. With his casual cruelty and his offhand treatment of her. She was required to respect him as her king, and even on some level as her parent. But that did not mean she was required to suffer his behavior for one moment more.

What was the worst that could happen? The King had already married her off to a stranger. Luc had already left her. There was no *worst*.

It was as if the sun had broken from behind the clouds.

Gabrielle raised her head and fastened her gaze on her father. It was as if she'd never seen him before. He was dressed, as ever, impeccably. His light brown hair was smoothed back from his aristocratic brow, and his handsome features were set in their usual expression of stern displeasure.

She had always disappointed him. Because she was not a boy. Because she was not able to read his mind, anticipate his needs. Because her mother had died and left her care in his hands. Because he was a man who would always be disappointed.

She remembered thinking that he was like Luc, that they were the same kind of man, and almost let out a laugh. The two men could not be more different. King Josef was petty, mean. Luc was elemental, unstoppable. King Josef dominated a room because he thought his consequence demanded it. Luc because he could not fail to do so—it was who he was, not what he did.

Most important, Luc had made her feel free. She had been more herself with him than she had ever been before. She hadn't had to be the constrained, quiet princess that King Josef demanded for Luc. Luc had liked it when she did not hide. He'd liked her wild, free—and only with Luc had she let herself be both proper in public and unrestrained in private.

Only with Luc…

"What do you have to smile about, may I ask?" King Josef asked, bristling. He put his silver fork down against his plate with a loud clunk. "When I think of the shame you have brought upon this family, this nation, I cannot imagine I will ever smile again."

"I was thinking of Luc," she said, her mind racing—the protective shell around her was broken now, and the feelings she'd been holding at bay were rushing in.

She had spent her whole life curling up into a ball, keeping her head down and staying silent, all in the desperate hope that she might please someone who could never be pleased. Why was she doing the same thing now? Why was she responding to Luc's anger as if he were her father?

"There is no point in wasting your time with Garnier," King Josef said dismissively. "He wants nothing to do with you."

"Yes, Father," Gabrielle said impatiently. Dismissively. "I was the one in the marriage. I know what he said."

A tense silence fell over the breakfast table. Gabrielle pulled herself away from her thoughts to notice that her father was staring at her, affront etched across every feature.

"I beg your pardon?" he said icily.

Ordinarily Gabrielle would have soothed him. Apologized to him. But then ordinarily his displeasure would have made her anxious—she would have felt horrible, fallen all over herself to fix things, yearned for some sign of approval or, barring that, no outward disapproval.

Today she found she didn't much care. She had finally had enough of trying to please him—enough of falling short.

"My marriage is none of your business," she told him. Quietly. Clearly. "I'll thank you to keep your opinions to yourself."

"Who do you think you are?" he demanded, puffing out his chest in outrage.

"I am the future queen of Miravakia," Gabrielle said, the words ringing out as if they'd been waiting years for her to voice them. She pushed her chair back from the table and stood tall. "If you cannot respect the fact that I am your daughter, and a grown woman, respect that."

"How *dare* you address me in this fashion?" King Josef barked. "Is this how you behaved during your association with Garnier? Is this why he washes his hands of you?"

"I think you mean my *marriage* to Luc Garnier," Gabrielle

corrected him gently, finding that after all this time she wasn't angry with her father. She was simply done with him. She looked at him and saw a very small man, crippled by his outsize sense of himself and his need to lord it over his own daughter.

"Your marriage is over," he shot back at her.

Gabrielle thought about that, carefully placing her snowy-white linen napkin next to her plate and stepping away from the table. Why was her marriage over? Because Luc said so? Well—who gave him that right? Even Luc Garnier could not so casually sunder what God had brought together. She had heard that much of her own wedding ceremony.

"Where are you going?" her father demanded as Gabrielle turned and headed for the door, a new resolve making her square her shoulders and spurring her into action.

She loved Luc. Their weeks apart had not altered that at all— if anything they had strengthened it. His horrible reaction had not lessened her feelings either, though she remained furious that he could so easily toss her aside. It was easy to see, in retrospect, that she and Luc had been played against each other by the noxious Silvio, and that Luc, predictably, had reacted with his usual high-octane fury. She was not sure she even blamed him—hadn't she known that any hint of scandal was Luc's worst nightmare? Apparently Silvio had known it, too.

But it was high time she stood up for herself. It was past time she went after what she wanted. She was not the weak, malleable creature she had been before. She had no intention of letting Luc walk away from her without a fight.

She would respond to Luc the way *he'd* responded to her when she'd run away from him.

She would hunt him down, explain to him that he had no other option, and take him to bed.

And when she thought about it in those terms she could hardly wait.

CHAPTER SEVENTEEN

ROME was hot and Luc was surly.

He skirted a group of Spanish-speaking tourists taking pictures of themselves in front of the Fontana del Nettuno at the northern end of the Piazza Navone, barely restraining himself from berating them simply for being in his way.

He was in a foul mood, and had been for weeks. He could not pretend he did not know why.

He had left Gabrielle in London, but her ghost followed him everywhere he went. First he had gone to Paris, where his business was headquartered. Work was his *raison d'être*. It had saved him when his parents died. It had defined his existence since. And yet he'd found himself unable to concentrate. He'd looked at contracts and thought of her mysterious smile, the one he had never decoded. He'd sat in meetings and imagined he was back in bed with her, wrapped up in her arms, their mouths and bodies fused together. He *felt* her—felt her hands upon his skin, felt the ways in which she had changed him—and he despaired that this was permanent, this emotional mess that he'd become.

He thought he might be going mad. Or, worse, was already mad.

He had removed himself to his home in Rome, a penthouse

apartment steps from the Piazza Navona. This was where he came to recharge his batteries. Though his mother's family maintained a villa on the Appian Way that had come to him upon her death, he had always preferred the bustle and endless motion of the city center.

Except for now. Rome, haunted by the ghosts of thousands of years, all of them indistinguishable beneath the Italian sky, now seemed haunted exclusively by the one woman Luc could not seem to escape. He saw her everywhere. He heard the music of her laughter on the breeze, glimpsed her face in every crowd and around every corner, and reached for her in his sleep only to wake, alone and furious.

No woman had ever gotten under his skin in this way.

No woman had ever gotten to him at all.

"I do not know when I will return," Luc growled into his mobile now, scowling at the usual frenzied scene spread out before him across the *piazza*. So many tourists and natives in the sun, enjoying the ease and flow of Roman life. And he, meanwhile, could not escape a woman he refused to allow himself to want any longer. She hung over Rome, the city of his heart and his youth, like a smog. She invaded him, altered him, and she was not even there.

"Capisco bene," Alessandro said over the phone. Too carefully. Too calmly. "I am capable of taking care of things at the office, Luc. You must take as much time as you need."

Luc realized that his second-in-command believed him to be nursing some kind of melodramatic romantic ailment, and let out a short laugh. How could he tell Alessandro that Gabrielle had managed to prise off the lid he had clamped down on emotions he had always denied he could ever feel? There was nothing melodramatic about it—it was all too inescapably mundane. And it was killing him.

"I am not lovesick, like a child, Alessandro," he snapped.

"Of course not," the other man replied. Obviously placating him.

It was enraging—yet Luc could do nothing but end the call.

He looked up as he approached his building, his scowl sharpening as he recognized the figure lurking near the haphazardly parked cars in front. The grizzled face and matted curls could belong to only one person: Silvio Domenico.

Exactly who Luc least wanted to see—ever, and certainly not in his current mood.

"Ah, Luc!" Silvio called, his voice heavy with mockery. "Such a beautiful day, is it not? Too bad you must spend it alone!"

As he spoke he lifted his camera and fired off a series of shots. Luc did not alter his stride as he approached—just as he did not alter his expression. The other man grinned at the sight—and not nicely.

"The strong, silent type today, eh?" he jeered. "No punches? No swearing? I am disappointed."

Luc closed the distance between them. He wanted to crush Silvio. He wanted to wrap his hands around the other man's throat, tear apart his limbs and throw them into the gutter for the dogs. But he did none of those things. He stopped, instead, when he was only a few feet away, and regarded the other man for a long, cool moment.

"I have yet to see my intimate life on the evening news," he said. "You disappoint me, Silvio."

"It's only a matter of time," the other man boasted. "There is nowhere you can go that I can't follow. Nothing you do that I won't record. No matter how rich and powerful you get, you still can't control me."

Luc waited for the usual wave of fury to crash through him, but it did not come. He thought instead of Gabrielle. He thought of the fact that no pictures had appeared anywhere—there were not even any rumors that embarrassing pictures existed, as there should have been. There was no whisper of any impropriety either in his marriage or concerning his wife. It dawned on Luc—slowly and inexorably—that there never would be.

That there had never been any photographs. There had only been Silvio, playing games, and Luc's immediate assumption that Gabrielle had betrayed him. Because everyone else had. He remembered with perfect, cutting clarity the way she had looked at him on that last evening—her eyes so wide, so dark, so filled with tears.

I love you. He heard her as clearly as if she stood behind him and whispered in his ear. *I love you.*

"Cat got your tongue?" Silvio taunted him, his lips curled.

"How tedious you are," Luc replied at length, when he was certain his voice would remain even. He eyed Silvio like the cockroach he was. "What an empty life you have made for yourself. I will endeavor to travel to more interesting places to give you a change of scenery, shall I?"

Silvio shot another round of pictures, sneering.

"Garnier, abandoned by wife, succumbs to drink and drug binge," he murmured. *"Once-feared multimillionare Garnier laid low by love—licks wounds in raunchy Roman orgy."*

Luc arched an eyebrow. "I never realized until this moment how obsessed you are with me," he murmured, feeling more like himself than he had in ages. "How sad."

"You should never have hit me!" Silvio snarled, with enough rage that Luc might have thought he referred to something that had occurred in the past decade, had he not known better.

"You should never have thrust your camera into a moment of private grief," Luc returned coolly. "Much less called my mother a whore."

"They say men marry their mothers," Silvio said, flashing a smile filled with yellow teeth and malice.

Luc's first urge was to plant his fist in Silvio's face—again. But that was reflex. When he thought about it for a moment, he nearly smiled. *I am not your mother*, Gabrielle had said. And indeed she was not. He realized now that she never had been.

"Are you calling my wife a whore?" he asked softly. He found he could not even feel the rage he ought to feel—because it was so patently absurd. Of *course* Gabrielle was an innocent. Luc was the only man who had ever touched her—he had taught her how to kiss!

"The Princess? I suppose not," Silvio murmured. "But she was so distraught at the idea of a sex tape of you and La Rosalinda that she paid me ten thousand pounds to destroy it." Silvio laughed. "As if I would turn over such a thing for so little, when it could make ten times that!"

Luc looked at him for a long moment. Could he blame Silvio? Or was it his fault for jumping to the conclusion that had supported his worst fears? She had not planned to embarrass him. There was no resemblance between Gabrielle and the others. No connection between her and the toad who stood before him. None.

"This is your revenge?" he asked at last.

"I don't need revenge," Silvio scoffed. "I have ten thousand pounds. Will you hit me again?" And now Silvio taunted him. "A broken nose this time, maybe? I wonder how much I can sue you for? A man can never have enough money."

Luc let out a laugh then. "There would be no point," he replied. He stepped around the little pig of a man and moved toward the front door of his building. "It is too absurd. By all means print that. Make a fool of yourself in front of all of Europe. With my compliments."

Silvio swore at him as he walked away, but Luc did not respond. He didn't care. It was as if Silvio had finally, after all these years of hunting him, ceased to exist.

He was far more focused on the fact that he'd called Gabrielle *my wife*. With no past tense.

Gabrielle arrived in Rome awash with memories.

It seemed like another person who had run to Rome from Miravakia in the wake of her own wedding—run from everything she knew and the man she most assuredly did not know.

How had so much changed in so little time? She was now bound and determined to fight for the man she had run from before. Her love for him seemed to burn inside her, bright and fierce and true, and it had nothing to do with how angry she was at the way he'd treated her. How had she changed so much—so much she hardly recognized herself?

Rome was the same. The boisterous, ebullient city surged around her as she rode in a taxi from the airport—unchanged and yet always changing, ancient and new, flexing its more than two thousand years of history and beauty in the Mediterranean sun. It had not taken too much work on her part to figure out where Luc had gone. He had told her himself that he preferred Rome above all other cities, though he only went there alone, and to unwind. Meaning he visited far less than he wished.

Gabrielle held tight to the fact that he was not in Paris, working—his second-in-command had told her so himself. Surely if she meant as little to Luc as he had claimed he would barely have noticed her absence? What was she to him, after all, but another in a long line of women? She could hardly expect to have dominated his world as he did hers—and his going back to work as if she had never existed would have been confirmation of that.

But the fact that he was not in France—that he did not even seem to be working—had to be a good thing, she told herself. It reminded her of something he'd told her during that lazy trip up the California coast.

They had been in Big Sur, awed by the giant trees and the craggy coastline. The Pacific Ocean had pounded against the rocks, swelling and retreating, churning up foam, far below the little cliffside path where they'd strolled.

"I will always prefer Rome to all other cities," he had said. "It is the place I am most at home."

"Why do you not go there more often?" she had asked. Hadn't he just said he spent little time there?

"My offices are in Paris," Luc had said matter-of-factly, shrugging, a faint frown between his eyes. As if he did not understand the question. As if there was nothing else that mattered but work.

Gabrielle remembered wondering why there was such a split in him—work and home forever on different sides of the divide. She had longed, then, to comfort him somehow—though she had sensed that he would not welcome it. Now she wondered why it had never occurred to her that he worked so hard, was so driven, because he knew nothing else. He did not even know he needed comfort.

She glanced down at her left hand, at the two rings that sat on her finger. The diamond he'd given her burst into flame and rainbow in the afternoon sun, reminding her of the night he'd presented it to her. He had been so stiff, so formal. So remote. Even then she had sensed his vulnerability—had known that even a man so powerful as Luc was uncertain. Was that when she had known that he must care for her, little though he might be able to show it?

Of course he could not trust her. He could not trust anyone. He had never had anyone to trust.

His parents had abandoned him—first to play their histrionic relationship games, then in dying so young. He had never allowed anyone else near. He'd had no reason not to believe it when Silvio made up lies about her—and if Gabrielle thought about what Luc had said, the references to *pictures*, she could imagine the form those lies had taken. She could not be surprised that Luc had felt so betrayed. A month or so of love could not cancel out the lifetime of distrust and suspicion that had preceded it.

It only made her more determined.

She would love him whether he wanted her to or not. She wouldn't stop just because he struck out at her, cast her aside. She loved him enough to know that she must never give up— she must break through, somehow, to that vulnerable part of him he kept hidden away. So that they could both be free— together.

Luc stood on the terrace of his penthouse, looking out over the rooftops of Rome. He had never brought one of his women to this place—the most private of his homes—and had had no specific intention to bring Gabrielle here, either, though he had married her.

Yet he couldn't seem to stop thinking of how much she would have loved to see the sun set over the city, creeping across the domes and steeples, the light orange and gold.

I love you.

He had called her *my wife*. Not *my ex-wife*. He had demanded that his lawyers draw up the necessary papers and then avoided their calls ever since. Today he had realized what he should have known all along—she had not betrayed him. That Silvio had played him for a fool, even played him against Gabrielle, and because he was a fool he had run with it. Embraced it. Had some part of him *wanted* to believe she was capable of such treachery? Had he *wanted* her to be his mother all over again? To confirm his darkest fears?

He couldn't seem to come to terms with what all of that meant. He who was famous for his decisiveness, his boldness.

He put his glass of wine down on the table and moved to the railing, restless. He remembered when he was younger, how he had stood in this same place and plotted the many ways he planned to increase his holdings, conquer his rivals, cut low his enemies. All of which he had done—in spades.

Now all he could think of was the mesmerizing curve of her hip, the small, pleading noise she made when she was close to her climax. Her serene, elegant smoothness and the wildness contained within it.

He was infatuated. Obsessed.

Even Rome seemed empty without her.

Luc was forced to admit defeat. It was a new and oddly uncomfortable experience.

But it seemed he could not live without her.

Had he already suspected as much in London? Was that why he'd been so quick to walk out on her? Had he been running for his life—the empty, emotionless life he had crafted so carefully and that she had destroyed forever?

He walked back into the flat from the terrace, scowling as he worked to come to terms with this new information. If he could not live without her, that meant that he had to get her back. It meant that, and it also meant a great many things he was not certain he wished to look at directly.

He turned when he heard the low chime of the elevator doors, opening inside his private foyer.

"I am so sorry, Mr. Garnier," the bellboy cried out immediately. "I know you ask that we announce all visitors, but this—"

"Hello, Luc," Gabrielle said quietly as she stepped from the elevator car.

Dio, but she was beautiful. She went straight to his head, standing there so composed and pretty, in a delicate blue jacket and skirt that he longed to rip from her body right there, tumbling them both to the marble floor.

"Gabrielle." He tasted the syllables of her name. Had he conjured her up? Had wanting her made her appear, like some genie from a childhood fairy tale?

He had showered after his run-in with Silvio, scrubbing the encounter off his skin. He'd thrown a button-down shirt on over his trousers, but neglected to fasten it—an impulse he was glad of as he watched the way her eyes caressed his chest and abdomen before they returned to his.

"I believe you forgot something," she said in her calm, soothing voice, her gaze intent on his as she stepped toward him. The elevator—dismissed with a wave of Luc's hand—closed behind her. "In your haste to get away."

He remembered his own words, delivered so differently, so angrily, a world away. He felt something like a smile curve his mouth.

"Did I?" he asked softly, drinking her in. "And what is that?"

She tossed her head back. Defiant, bold. She was different than he remembered—more vibrant, more sure. She looked him in the eye. She was not afraid.

She was glorious.

"Your wife," she said.

CHAPTER EIGHTEEN

"I LOVE you," she told him, marching across the marble foyer and stopping when she was only inches from his hard, beloved face. "Even though you broke my heart in London. I love you, and I refuse to accept that our marriage is over."

"You have grown claws, it seems," Luc murmured in that silky way of his. "I see my absence has suited you."

She couldn't read his expression. There was something new in the way he looked at her—but it was not cold, or vicious. Hope unfurled inside her chest and mingled with the determination that had already guided her here.

"It did not suit me." She found that her hands were on her hips. "You were an ass."

His lips curved. "I thought you sold Silvio photographs," Luc said. "Compromising photographs from our honeymoon, to be precise."

He spoke rather too mildly, Gabrielle thought with asperity. But then, he did not dispute the fact that he'd been an ass.

"I paid him for a tape of you and that Rosalinda—to prevent his selling it," Gabrielle shot back. She frowned as his words penetrated. "Photographs of you and *me*?"

"You sound appalled," Luc said.

"Of course I'm appalled!" Gabrielle retorted. "How could

you believe such a thing? I would never sell photographs to anyone—I am the Crown Princess of Miravakia! I am not some second-rate starlet!"

"I know who you are," he said, his eyes darkening.

"Clearly not!"

He cocked his head to the side and she stared back, her hands fisted on her hips. The air around them seemed to seethe with tension. Heat. Gabrielle's eyes felt overbright, her cheeks were too warm, and she felt as if the room was spinning, whirling. All that she could see was Luc's steady, addictive gray gaze.

"I know exactly who you are," he said, his voice a low throb that seemed to echo in her chest, along her limbs, between her legs. "You haunt me."

He looked like some kind of warrior, some avenging angel, his face resolute and fierce—and the most beautiful thing that Gabrielle had ever seen.

"I know your voice because I cannot escape it," he told her in a savage tone. "I know your touch because I dream of it. I know your scent, your voice, your walk." His voice faded away into almost nothing, the faintest whisper of sound. And yet he held himself away from her.

"Had you only talked to me about his accusations—" Gabrielle began, frowning at him even as her breath came quicker, in little pants, and her attention focused on his dangerous mouth.

"I could not," Luc said fiercely. Such a proud, difficult man. His gaze turned almost defiant. "I did not know how. And it seems he knew how best to manipulate us both."

If possible, she loved him more for the admission. She could feel the change in him, though she hardly dared dream what it might mean. He stood before her like some kind of Roman god, his chiseled torso gleaming, his dark hair thick and damp, his eyes so dark, like steel, and his cruel, delicious mouth pulled to the side in a sardonic smile.

"Why are you here?" Luc asked, his voice still and quiet, with the faintest hint of mockery. As if he knew already. "Did you hunt me down?"

"I will not grant you a divorce. I will fight an annulment. I'll fight *you*," she said, tilting her chin up.

"Why?" he asked. He moved closer, his glorious chest now within reach, his mouth a bare whisper above hers, his dark eyes boring into her, seeing into her—through her.

"Because I love you," she said softly. "Why else?"

"Ah, love," he said, hardly above a whisper. "Is that what it is? How do you know?"

"You have ruined me for other men," she told him, tilting her head back, easing ever closer, not daring to touch him but almost—almost…

"Have you tested the theory?" he asked sardonically, but his eyes gleamed with amusement.

"And if I had?" she asked, teasing him. She was not sure where her sudden sense of daring came from. She only knew that she dared. She dared anything and everything if she could have him.

"Ah, Gabrielle," he muttered, his voice thickening as he thrust a strong hand into her heavy hair, anchoring her head against his hot palm and drawing her up on her toes. "You will be the death of me."

"You love me," she said simply. She knew it deep inside, as much a fact as her need to breathe, as her own love for him.

There was a breathless, electric pause. Luc stared at her. She slid her hands around his strong neck and arched into him, pressing her aching breasts against him. He groaned, deep in his throat.

"I do, damn you," he said in a low voice, his eyes nearly silver. "I do."

His mouth covered hers, and Gabrielle surrendered herself

to the kick and roll, the heat and wonder. He kissed her again and again, savage and tender, as if he could never get enough. It was an apology, and it was a covenant, and she could not tell where she ended and he began.

He bent slightly and swept her into his arms, never lifting his mouth from hers. Gabrielle had the faintest hectic impression of an elegantly appointed drawing room before he deposited her on the Oriental rug in front of a fireplace and followed her down—and then his hard chest crushed into her with delicious pressure.

Gabrielle groaned—and forgot about the room. She didn't care where they were. She cared only that she was touching him—finally. His hands stroked her, moving to her hips and hiking up her skirt so she could wrap her legs around his waist.

She struggled with the zip of his trousers and he cursed slightly. He shifted and released himself with two quick jerks. She had only a dizzy moment to look at his manhood, jutting proudly before him, and then he was thrusting into her, deep and hard and wild, and she thought no more.

She came almost instantly, shuddering around him. Luc felt the dark sorcery of her taste, her touch, overwhelm him, and he followed, shouting out her name.

But it was not magic, he knew, as he slowly came back to himself. It was love.

No wonder he had cast it aside and run from it—just as she had done in the beginning. No wonder he had so quickly grasped any excuse to leave her.

"What I know of love is twisted," he told her when her eyes fluttered open. He traced patterns along the sweat-slick skin of her thigh, still wrapped around him. "Sick."

"Then it is not love," she whispered, her sea-colored eyes calm as she regarded him.

"I do not believe in it," he said. He kissed her brow, the tip of her nose, her cheek. "I don't know how to believe in it."

"It's not in your head, but in your heart." She placed one of her slender hands on his chest. He felt his heart kick beneath her touch. "I spent my whole life loving someone who cannot love me in return," she said. "I think love is feeling free. Not hidden away, not afraid. But finally whole—together."

She was wondrous. She was his wife. He felt a deep, primal surge of possession and emotion and knew she was right. He loved her.

Beyond rationale and reason, he was madly in love with her. Crazy with it. And the most insane part was that he no longer cared that he had lost his objectivity.

"I love you," he said fiercely, testing it out, even as he hardened once more within her. He scowled at her. "And I do not think it will ever change. I do not think you will escape it."

"Good," she whispered, and began to move her hips against him.

It would always be this way, Gabrielle thought some time later. She was wrapped in his long shirt and in his arms, enjoying the glittering Rome night from his balcony. She leaned back into his embrace, smiling.

There would be no ordinary Thursdays in their marriage, there would be only Luc. He would not be easy, and perhaps she would not be either. But they would have this passion— this wild, sweet fire that burned them both into ash—again and again. She wanted him still—again. Always.

"I will get back what you paid that little toad," Luc promised her suddenly. She could feel his voice rumble in his chest and through her. "He will not profit from my wife for a tape that does not exist. To the tune of ten thousand pounds, no less!"

"I don't care about it," Gabrielle murmured, tilting her head back to nestle against him. "I never even looked at it."

"I care." His voice was implacable. "It is the principle. He will no doubt turn it into another series of stories, but that is of no matter to me. Let him. But he *will* pay you back the money he extorted, this I promise you."

Gabrielle smiled. If he no longer cared about the tabloids, then things really had changed. What had started as a vain hope mixed with a deep resolve, and had bloomed during their impassioned lovemaking, now burst into light inside her.

They would make it. It would be all right. This was as it should be—finally.

"If you wish it," she said.

"How can you love such a man as me?" he asked her, his tone deceptively light. When she turned to face him, his eyes were hard on hers. "One who abuses you so terribly, chases you and then abandons you, believes the worst of you, accuses you of every sin imaginable?"

Gabrielle reached over and laid her hand against his cheek, making both of them take a quick, startled breath in response to the electric heat that arced between them, as if they had not made love three times already. She traced the shape of his lean jaw, then curled her fingers around his neck.

She would love this man forever.

"Well, Luc," she said, and smiled, letting him see all the light and hope and love she carried inside her. "See that it does not happen again."

He muttered a soft curse, or perhaps it was her name, and crushed his mouth to hers.

And Gabrielle knew beyond a shadow of a doubt that they had both found their way home.

At last.

millsandboon.co.uk Community

Join Us!

The Community is the perfect place to meet and chat to kindred spirits who love books and reading as much as you do, but it's also the place to:

- ■ Get the inside scoop from authors about their latest books
- ■ Learn how to write a romance book with advice from our editors
- ■ Help us to continue publishing the best in women's fiction
- ■ Share your thoughts on the books we publish
- ■ Befriend other users

Forums: Interact with each other as well as authors, editors and a whole host of other users worldwide.

Blogs: Every registered community member has their own blog to tell the world what they're up to and what's on their mind.

Book Challenge: We're aiming to read 5,000 books and have joined forces with The Reading Agency in our inaugural Book Challenge.

Profile Page: Showcase yourself and keep a record of your recent community activity.

Social Networking: We've added buttons at the end of every post to share via digg, Facebook, Google, Yahoo, technorati and de.licio.us.

www.millsandboon.co.uk

2 FREE BOOKS
AND A SURPRISE GIFT

We would like to take this opportunity to thank you for reading this Mills & Boon® book by offering you the chance to take TWO more specially selected books from the Modern™ series absolutely FREE! We're also making this offer to introduce you to the benefits of the Mills & Boon® Book Club™—

- **FREE home delivery**
- **FREE gifts and competitions**
- **FREE monthly Newsletter**
- **Exclusive Mills & Boon Book Club offers**
- **Books available before they're in the shops**

Accepting these FREE books and gift places you under no obligation to buy, you may cancel at any time, even after receiving your free books. Simply complete your details below and return the entire page to the address below. You don't even need a stamp!

YES Please send me 2 free Modern books and a surprise gift. I understand that unless you hear from me, I will receive 4 superb new books every month for just £3.19 each, postage and packing free. I am under no obligation to purchase any books and may cancel my subscription at any time. The free books and gift will be mine to keep in any case.

Ms/Mrs/Miss/Mr_____ Initials _____

Surname _____

Address _____

_____

_____ Postcode _____

Send this whole page to: Mills & Boon Book Club, Free Book Offer, FREEPOST NAT 10298, Richmond, TW9 1BR.